The World's First Ever Baptist Crime Novel

By
George Breed & Ginny Stewart

iUniverse, Inc.
New York   Bloomington

iUniverse books may be ordered through booksellers or by contacting:

iUniverse
1663 Liberty Drive
Bloomington, IN 47403
www.iuniverse.com
1-800-Authors (1-800-288-4677)

ISBN: 978-1-4401-2764-9 (sc)
ISBN: 978-1-4401-2765-6 (ebook)

Printed in the United States of America

iUniverse rev. date: 03/19/2009

Table of Contents

Acknowledgments

I thank the Muse I know so well, who said so clearly "Write a Baptist Crime Novel," and my sister Ginny who gave initial strong encouragement and then joined in as co-author so enthusiastically (and at times with understandable trepidation as we recalled old ghosts) as we followed what unfolded with surprise and glee. Often we were exhausted at the end of a chapter as we not only wrote it but lived it as we wrote.

Rose Hauk gave us an early thumbs up and some valuable suggestions after being the first other person to read the manuscript. Kathy Aycock, my shy sister who loves to live way outside of any town of any size, was in on the beginning plot and gave some fruitful ideas.

Ken McIntosh, after learning of the manuscript's existence during our weekly breakfasts and metaspiritual discussions, kept asking to read it and finally I was wise enough to hand it over. Ken gave powerful encouragement and feedback ranging from character development to the proper placement of quotation marks. Though a busy man, he took the time.

I appreciate Kato the cat who sat looking at me with patient puzzlement when my fingers would not leave the keyboard to get his food. He rules the house and granted me, his servant, his tolerance and forgiveness.

My friend, artist extraordinaire and book cover designer, Cathy Gazda, who lives down the road in Sedona came through once again with an original cover, the fourth she has designed for me and I hope there are many more.

My partner, Karen, as always, gave loving support and understanding and even allowed me to occasionally beat her in a game of SkipBo during writing intermissions.

--George Breed

While considering those to thank for their part in helping me write this book, I realized the one I am most thankful to is God, my heavenly Father. Without Him we can do nothing.

Kathy Aycock, my precious sister and confidante, gave us some very helpful suggestions on the beginning plot when I was stuck for ideas. After her help I was off and running.

Peggy and Marion Hammond, who are very dear friends, have both been very supportive. Marion is a master woodworker as well as assistant pastor of our church and yet took the time to read the manuscript and give us his thoughts and suggestions. Peggy is one of the most pleasant, positive thinking people I've known. She just kept encouraging me and filling me with her wonderful southern cooking.

Jaime Davis is the mother of my youngest grandchild. She excels in everything she does. Her encouraging and uplifting words kept me writing when I lacked self-confidence. I was often inspired by the thought of leaving my granddaughter, Lilly, a written legacy of some of what her grandmother's life was like.

My husband, Dave, as always was my most supportive fan. As is his usual nature, he was patient and understanding. Many times he took care of the details of life for me while I tapped away on the keyboard.

It goes without saying that my brother, George Richard, gave me confidence to continue writing when I thought I couldn't. After all, if an author of several books tells you that you have talent, how could I argue? This time of writing with him has caused a refocusing of how I view my life.

--Ginny Stewart

Preface

by George Breed

Here is how *The World's First Ever Baptist Crime Novel* brought itself into life. It began in my deciding to not *make* anything happen for a while, to *not* restart another round of Warrior of Spirit weekly meetings, to *not* apply to conferences and gatherings as a speaker / workshop leader, to *not* put myself out there in any *form*.

Rising in the pre-dawn every morning and sitting quietly, as is my wont, I fully expected that at some point, the word of my new marching orders would come. Four weeks went by. Five. I was prepared to sit for at least a year and was enjoying the silent bliss. Then it came. Pre-dawn. Quietly sitting. Still small Voice: *"Write a Baptist Crime Novel."* "**What!?**" Again: *"Write a Baptist Crime Novel."*

I sat there laughing, almost giggling. I thought, *"You've got to be kidding!"* but I knew from experience not to ask a third time. One just gets the same answer. I shook my head in bemusement as I walked over to the computer keyboard. *"Alright, I will."* Within an hour, I had written four chapters.

I decided to email my sister. I didn't tell her of the Voice at first.

January 18, 2008

Hi Ginny, I never heard of a Baptist crime novel so I thought I might write one. Here is the opening -- hot off my scalded brain.

January 19, 2008

Hey to you!!! Very interesting reading. I do believe I have met some of the characters in your crime novel. They sure sound familiar. I loved it! Altar ego? Still laughing at that one. You have quite a gift. Continue on in this novel and send me the chapters as you finish them. I haven't read anything this good in a long time.

Glad you like the writing. I like it as it unfolds, gets me to chortling, snuculating, and guffawing, but that doesn't mean anyone else will like it. It's best to write for one's own amusement I find. That way there's always a gain.

Write for your amusement if you like, but send material on to me. This is something that anyone would enjoy. Looking forward to more. Chortling, snuculating, and guffawing as I reread it.

January 20, 2008

Okay, Girl. You asked for it. Chapter First, which you already received, is entitled **Spittle, Theology, and The Worm.** Here is Chapter Second -- **Sweaty Fervent Hands, Deacons Wives, and Lottie Moon**

I'm loving it! While I read this I have the mental picture of (xxxxx) in mind. More, please. Can't wait to see where this is going.

January 21, 2008

Good Morning, Ginny. (xxxxx)? Hmmm… wonder what gave you that idea? Here is the next installment in this saga – **Luther Huckleberry**

Okay, you have so wonderfully set the scene for several plots. I can't wait to see how they develop. My curiosity is having fits. What blood does the preacher have on his hands? What about the youth minister's sermon? What's up with Millie and the preacher? Luther is surely to do something wild as this progresses, but what? Write fast…….

Okay, Ginny. Here's the next installment – **Restless Dog**

Ginny, I done got me an idea. If you are of a mind, write a short chapter on Millie Huckleberry. I don't know what she is like yet. So it's wide open.

Okay. It may take me some time. And it may not.

Yes!

Well, glory be! I put these fingers on the keyboard and my mind took over. Here comes Millie! Let me know what you think. – **Millie Huckleberry**

Hey! Just got in from a long walk. This is wonderful! I think you are doing what I am doing -- just listening to the inner voice. Was thinking we could write **The First Ever Baptist Crime Novel** together. Kind of interweave our thinking and see what unfolds. I have no idea how this is going to turn out. I'm just letting it unfold. Novelists have said their characters just take over with a life of their own. We have five here so far. Millie, the Preacher, Luther, the Youth Minister, Some Bozo Narrator. Want to keep playing and see what happens?

*   *   *

And off we went, writing most every day. At first, writing individual chapters without conferring with each other; then, fairly quickly, writing many of the succeeding chapters together in our email chat room. We had a general idea of what might happen in a chapter but we were often surprised. The characters took over and refused to obey our will. We relented and let them have their lives.

This is a strange book. It literally asked to be written. It is published here roughly in the order in which it arose. It refuses to be wrestled into, forced into, any other template. It tells of humans, angels, demons, mobsters and their interactive attempts to control the world they live in. A spiritual criminologist and a shaman come to help sort things out.

A range of metaphysical views meet and clash and sometimes merge with understanding. Stubbornness of mindset is encountered on all "sides" and dealt with but never fully resolved. People are who they are and do not easily transform. Forced into a situation, however, which affects everyone's wellbeing produces an alchemical furnace into which everyone is thrown. Attempts are then made to change leaden ways into fluid gold. Something similar is happening in our world today.

Preface

by Ginny Stewart

The title of this book, 'The World's First Ever Baptist Crime Novel', can give the reader several different ideas of the contents of this book depending on your background and beliefs. Since this is a cooperative writing effort between my brother and me, you will find varying beliefs within. Also, you will find similar overall beliefs.

The obvious gist of the story is that of a murder committed in a Baptist church and the solving of that crime. Another more important essence of our writing is the revealing of crimes committed in the name of religion against people by some who consider themselves far above anyone else. This opinion is based solely on their ability to push other people around. Humbleness and thoughts for the welfare of others are not found anywhere in their lifestyle. These are people who base their life on a show of religion and not on a personal relationship with God and His Son, Jesus Christ. Much harm has been done to individuals by these religious bullies. So much so that some victims have vowed to distance themselves from any form of religion. Some see these bullies as God's henchmen and therefore run screaming from anyone who even speaks His name. God is not involved in any of their mistreatment of others and is not even remotely like that. But the only way you will find that out is to seek Him for yourself. Read His Word and find out how He feels about this kind of conduct and, more importantly, how He feels about you.

The fact that this all occurs in a Baptist church is not a condemnation of the Baptist denomination. Hypocrisy is not found solely among Baptists. Hypocrisy occurs among people who claim to know a God that they do not know. Knowing God is free to all who seek Him and is provided by the selfless sacrifice of His Son.

I believe the Bible is the inspired Word of God. The truths within His Word are not *my* truths, but *His* truths. Those truths have the ability to change a person. You will see a transformation in some of the characters of this book. Some change when they realize that God has not left them in charge of others to decide their worth or their fate. Others change when they come to realize their own worth. God did not assign us the position of being lord over others or the doormat of anyone.

List of Characters:

Charley - Youth minister, somewhat innocent and naïve, but learning

The Reverend Milton T. Bagston - Reprobate; scoundrel without whom there would be no story

Millie Huckleberry - Another naive innocent who begins to awaken to the peculiarities of life and finds that her life is not as she imagined

Luther Huckleberry - Lives according to his own lights, outside the bounds of conventional morality of the church; good friend of Charley; Millie's brother

Janice Bagston - The Reverend's wife who comes into her own after his death

Jeanine Bulloch - A somewhat tight-assed "real Christian" who loosens up some along the way

Ted Wilson - An intellectual free-thinker; initially Jeanine's spiritual arch-enemy; is also Charley's mentor

Viola Trumpett - A spiritual criminologist who looks to solve the mystery of Bagston's death

Florence/Flo - A complex woman who owns a Glock and knows how to use it; plays a strong part in Millie's life

Gregor - A demon from hell

Thelma - A former stripper with a low I.Q. and a good heart

Junior - Thelma's significant other

The Light - A personification of the light of consciousness

The Angel of Fire - A personification of the burning energy of being

Freddy Tempest - A hooligan for the mob

Little Jimmie Gallup - Narcissistic evangelical preacher

Miss Evelyn - Sanctimonious somewhat ditzy church member and baker of spurned cookies

Henry Wide Bear - Creek shaman and friend of Viola

Phil Rock Boy - Lakota Sioux; friend and assistant of Henry Wide Bear

The World's
First Ever
Baptist
Crime Novel

Restless Dog

When Brother Bagston preached, you could see the spittle fly if you were sitting to the side in the choir and the sun shone just right through the window.

Lord! When would he get done?

The women were fanning away with their cardboard fans, the ones with Jesus praying in the garden on the front and the back saying Hudson-Bailey was your best bet, the only bet really, for the maximum grave experience.

It was the P words that got the most trajectory. The folk in the front row were getting baptized and didn't seem to know it. Sprinkled really. Hmmm.... wasn't sprinkling a Methodist thing? My mind reeled at the theological implications. Would a Methodist-type sprinkling of Full-Dunk Baptists given and received unawares count as a sacrament? Holy Spit!

Wups! Everybody was standing up now for altar call. I stood too. Yep, here she came. Miss Evelyn. Right on cue. She always came during the invitational hymn. She had an altar ego.

And so I amused himself on Sunday mornings. I already had all the sermons memorized and would experiment with different endings than the one the expectorator would inevitably give. Like Joan and the Worm instead of Jonah and the Whale.

It was funny how folk always focused on God preparing the Whale, but not on his preparing the Worm. Right there in the Bible too. It was like a magician trick. Put the attention on the Whale and the Worm would just slide by.

Kind of like the preacher did with Millie Huckleberry.

I was the only one who knew about the preacher and the blood that stained his hands. And it wasn't the Blood of Jesus either.

I did not like the preacher and what he stood for. I am guilty of the sin of haughtiness and pride. I know that everything I saw in him and detested has a seed, a germ that if watered would flourish within me.

And yet, what he did was wrong. I know that.

I was going through what the mystics of all faiths call the dark night of the soul. It seems to come after a period of great illumination. And I'd had that. And now this.

I was like a dog turning round and round before it flops down on its resting place.

Except I could no longer find the resting place.

The church had gotten too small for my soul. Martin Buber said that religion "rests on an enormous simplification of the manifold and wildly engulfing forces that invade us." I was feeling the truth of that.

The preacher said that was where I fell into trouble in the first place, going to night school and then to evening college, getting exposed to those ideas that ran contrary to God's teachings in the King James version of the Bible.

Maybe he was right, but I don't think so. I was doomed from early on to exploration of all bounds. Tomorrow's heaven always rested on today's reality. And I felt the bounds of today's reality were manufactured, then accepted, by those less adventurous. I think Jesus came to tell us this. But that's another story.

With my beginning to see the preacher's version of the universe as grade school teachings and looking to move on to junior high, I found myself, to continue the analogy, staying outside at recess more and more, and in my mind, though my body continued to attend, skipping school altogether.

Though I wasn't into naked women and discharging shotguns, Luther Huckleberry and I were more alike than others might think. We both had trouble with boundaries. And so did the preacher.

Lest you think I am just a self-righteous finger-pointer, I tell you this up front right now, in recounting this story, I tell the state of my own soul.

Sweaty Fervent Hands, Deacon's Wives, and Lottie Moon

It was Youth Sunday and so, being a full-blooded youth, Charley was invited to give the sermon. Not much the preacher could do about it, since the deacon's wives pushed for it as a group.

He could run with the men. On Tuesday-Night-Home-Visitation running with them as a pack, surrounding poor backsliding church members in their own living room, laying sweaty fervent hands upon them, and praying for their soul.

Standing with the men on the church steps between Sunday School and the Morning Service while they smoked, kidded each other, and talked politics, the weather, and ball scores.

Yep. He could hang out with the men, but it was the women who wanted to hear him speak. They said when he talked they could feel the Spirit. And each of them wanted him to genetically couple with one of their daughters. All in the proper fashion of course. None of this backseat of a car panting and groping.

The church service had followed the traditional Baptist format, been through the hymn singing, the offering, and the announcements (remember the Lottie Moon offering coming up in a month).

The choir had sung its song, the solo part done by Grace Rudebaker in her fine voice, quavering and vibrating at the end of each long-held note, looking to break all wine-glasses in the vicinity and finding none since the church used solid shot glasses for its Welch's grape juice communion, knowing, unlike the poor benighted Catholics, that the juice did not really turn into Christ's blood, and if you spilled some on your shirt that did not make it a holy relic.

He had given his texts, the people dutifully following along in their King James Bibles --*For in him we live and move and have our being* (Acts 17: 28) and *The kingdom of God is within you* (Luke 17:21) and started his sermon.

That is when all hell broke loose.

Charley's Sermon

"When you first come out of the muck, you feel real happy.

No muck, no more, you say.

And you start making a sharp distinction between Muck and Not-Muck.

And that's the first mistake, though understandable. Because you certainly don't want to fall back into the muck. Your muck-detector is turned way up high.

And yet, being muck-sensitive, on high muck-alert, that means you are still caught up in the muck.

If you are going to make distinctions, the distinction to make is between Muck and Radiance."

He could feel the preacher behind him squirming and shuffling in his seat. That meant the preacher thought Charley was moving onto questionable theological ground.

But Charley had chosen his backup scripture wisely and pressed on.

"And what is Radiance? It is knowing, knowing not just with your head, in fact your head can't quite understand it, but knowing deep within your heart that you are in God and God is in you.

Just like it says in Acts 17 and Luke 17 in the passages we just now read together."

The preacher sounded like he was having phlegm trouble, coughing and blowing his nose. He knew where Charley was headed with this. They had had conversations, if you can call explosive angry outbursts conversations, about this before.

Charley continued with his sermon.

"When you walk around looking at what is Muck and what is Not-Muck, you are going to get all pious and holy. You are going to stink of holiness. You will stink to high heavens, so that even God himself will be holding his nose."

The congregation laughed. They understood what pious holiness smelled like.

"But when you walk through the day knowing that you are in God and God is in you, you will be Radiant. No muck in sight. Not a single sign of muck. No judgments on your fellow humans about their degree of muckiness. No distinction between Baptists and Methodists, between Baptists and Presbyterians, between Baptists and Catholics, between Baptists and Hindus, between WhateverName and WhateverName, because you are Radiant! Radiant! (Charley was on a full roll now.)

Because you are in God and God is in you!"

BLAM! The preacher jumped up so hard and furious he knocked his pulpit chair over.

Enraged at Charley's words, Bagston leaped from his chair, knocking it over in his zeal, went off balance, one foot tripping over the other, launched himself through the air, and hit head first on the "This Do In Remembrance Of Me" solid oak altar table just below the pulpit.

Those present would remember the sickening sound for years to come, a loud CRACK like dry furniture suddenly splitting combined with a THUNK as if a ripe watermelon had been hit with an axe handle.

Dead on the spot.

Oddly appropriate, sprawled across the communion table, his body and his blood.

Luther Huckleberry

Now the Huckleberrys, the tribe from which Millie sprang, were decent folk though considered a little too rural for the town folks' liking. The Huckleberry fashion statement was overalls for the men and shapeless cotton dresses for the women, who wore no bras for ease of teat access to their suckling brood.

Both men and women loved their tobacco, the men chewing and the women dipping, all carrying spit cans when in the house for any length of time, especially in the evenings when the men would play dominos and sip fine clear moonshine out of jelly glasses, and the women would be shelling peas in their aproned laps and listening to the gospel hour on the radio.

Of all the Huckleberrys, Luther was considered the wildest.

Luther Huckleberry was a man not much given to convention. Some folk said he was entirely unreasonable, but my take on him was that he just had reasons of his own.

He certainly didn't seem to care what the God-fearing Baptists of the town thought or didn't think. He seemed to pay us no mind at all.

His latest exploit, which passed from tongue to tongue like a scandalous French-kissing bug, was to be seen late one night riding through town with a naked woman (a good old girl from Hogansville it was said) sitting by his side in his old beatup Ford. The town women were scandalized. The men were appreciative and envious, silently of course.

And then there was the time he blew a hole with his choked-down shotgun through a drinking buddy's front door. Luther was never charged. Though there were many hypotheses, I think the buddy had crossed some kind of line and Luther, like any well-bred pirate, was simply firing a warning shot across his buddy's bow. In any event, they never seemed to have any trouble with each other after that.

As I got to know Luther better, I realized he didn't think these or any of the other things attributed to him were exploits at all. He was just living his life.

Luther was Millie's oldest brother.

Theologian Meets Beologian

Luther had been in the military, the U.S. Marines to be exact, laughing all the way.

Luther had found no gig, no role large enough to hold him. He was always moving on, refusing to even consider living a life of boredom. When a friend asked if he wasn't concerned about security, Luther looked puzzled, then lit up with laughter. "There is no such thing as security," he grinned, seeming mightily pleased about it. "And that means there is security everywhere!" The friend didn't get it, but Luther didn't seem to mind.

That was another thing about Luther. He wasn't trying to convert anyone to anything. A whole different creature was Luther, living in a community where everyone was trying to get everyone else to adopt their point of view. Each was convinced that if you followed their recipe for living, you would wind up with the best soup of all. Trouble was when you looked at their lives, one kind of lost one's appetite.

Luther and Charley were buddies since that morning that brought them together. They saw life in a similar fashion though one of them was considered by folk to be a pagan heathen and the other a staunch Christian (even though a little peculiar sometimes in his understandings of the scriptures).

Luther told Charley he didn't know anything about theology.

"I'm more into Be-ology! he said. "The study of Being itself. And no book study either. Full immersion. That's the only way to understand Being. You know what I mean. You Baptizers believe in full immersion."

"But Luther, we mean in the church. It's holy and it's sacred and it means coming up new and fresh and leaving the old behind."

"Perzackly! It's the same in Be-ology. Hell, boy! All of this is church." He waved his hands and arms around indicating the countryside around them. "Not just that little old building y'all have downtown."

Luther was getting warmed up now. "It's all holy. It's all sacred. And we are fully immersed and coming up new all the time! It's not just church on Wednesday night and Sunday. It's Church all the time!"

Charley grinned. "Does anybody else know you think this way?"

"No. Most folk keep their distance. Except for you, out here running around with renegades and sinners. What's that all about?"

"Well, Luther, I think people are scared of you."

"And why is that, Charley?"

"Because they are afraid of themselves."

Spiritual Jail

Charley and Luther were down by the river. Or what used to be the river until the government put a series of dams on it, turning it into a chain of "recreational areas".

Luther said, "If you can't do the crime, don't do the time."

"What? Luther, don't you have that backwards?"

"Nope."

"Well, what does that mean? That doesn't make any sense, Luther!"

"What do you think it means?"

"Hummmm"... (Silence) ...."That folk keep themselves imprisoned for no reason?"

"Yep. And on the bright side of it, if you are not going to commit spiritual crimes against people, and for sure, if you are not going to be a spiritual criminal, you won't be a physical one, there's no need to lock yourself up in your tight little jail cell of a mind."

"What you are saying is you can trust yourself to say and do the right thing. It will just come out naturally."

"Yep."

"Well, Luther, how can you be sure you won't commit spiritual crimes against people?"

"Lovingkindness, me bucko, lovingkindness. It's like the samurai used to say: The best defense is complete vulnerability. And lovingkindness is the most vulnerable place of all."

"I see. If you are walking around totally vulnerable, you won't be hurting anybody."

"Yes, and the funny thing about it is that being totally vulnerable is the strongest position of all. Why, look at your Jesus! Lovingkindness, Charley, lovingkindness!"

Millie Huckleberry

The Huckleberry clan was mighty proud of the fact that they didn't exactly fit into polite society. They saw being misfits as some kind of badge of honor, entirely different than how the prim and proper Baptist congregation saw them. I can't imagine a worse fate in life than that borne by poor Millie Huckleberry. She was truly a misfit among misfits. She didn't feel like she rightly belonged anywhere.

Millie was the only member of her family who attended the Baptist church. In fact, she was the only one who darkened the door of any church. Even there she was looked down on because of who spawned her. Except by the oh so religious Bro. Bagston. Now, his attention to Millie was not from the love in his heart but the lust in his eye. Millie was a right handsome young woman, but in her lowness of spirit she didn't recognize it.

Being a victim of her own mind, Millie believed whatever she was told. If she was told she was plain, then that was the gospel truth. If she was told she was lazy, then all the hard work in the world would make no difference. She wished so hard for approval somewhere, but never found it. She wasn't as smart as the men in her family and certainly not as adventurous as her older brother Luther. How she longed to be more like him, not caring what anybody thought. How could anyone live up to Luther's example? What was his example anyway? I don't think even Luther knew what he was going to do from one minute to the next.

Millie wished she could talk to someone about her vexation of mind. But the Huckleberry's had a long history of keeping family secrets and thoughts to yourself. Revealing family happenings had a penalty that went with it. She didn't exactly know what it was, but she didn't want to find out. Although there was Miss Florence over at the 5 and 10 that Millie came close to discussing her personals with. Most of the townspeople called her Flo, but Millie didn't feel very comfortable with that.

Giving consideration to her own opinions just never occurred to Millie. After all, if no one ever listens to your opinion, you figure you don't have one. She held in high regard, almost feared, anyone with authority over her. She was taught this from birth as were the other females in her family. One's position in life was enough to make Millie think that they were beyond reproach. Thus, her relationship with Bro. Bagston. She had fallen prey to his amorous pursuits, mistaking them for some sort of validation. It felt good to be thought a worthy companion for such a lofty man of God. But her stringent upbringing told her that this path leads straight to eternity in hell.

It was the preacher's idea to have Millie do some part-time secretarial work at the church. This would give him easy access to her and provide more opportunities to convince her that a union between them was designed by God himself. There, as she went about her duties, she began to pick up on some things in the life of Bro. Bagston that didn't exactly smell right. Her desk was right outside his study. She began to identify the callers he had, whether on the phone or in person. The walls were so thin that she could overhear the conversations whether she wanted to or not. She struggled with this in her conscience, but soon became so wrapped up in the goings-on that she couldn't help herself.

Millie had never been taught anything about the business world. It wasn't exactly the topic of conversation at the Huckleberry dinner table. If she had, she could have understood what the hollering was all about when the chairman of the deacon board met with Bagston about the church bonds. "Misappropriation of funds" was something she knew nothing about. But she did know a mad deacon when she saw one, especially as he exited the pastor's study muttering under his breath about someone having to pay. The slamming of the door as he left took away all doubt that he was serious.

The pastor's wife hardly ever visited the church during the week. She was caught up in her Missionary Society work. She and the other good women of the church had little to do at home, so they busied themselves with the Lord's work. "Do-gooders" Millie's Papa would call them. Luther had other names for them, but Millie couldn't repeat them.

Millie's Quandary

Bro. Bagston's death was heavy on the minds of the townsfolk, not to mention the good people of the Baptist church. Services had been called off. No one could bring themselves to worship in a sanctuary where the carpet was still stained with the blood of their leader. They couldn't even discuss forming a pulpit committee to find the church another pastor. After all, there should be a respectable period of mourning, shouldn't there?

Not everyone felt charitable about Bagston. Certainly not the chairman of the deacon board, and not Miss Florence at the 5 and 10. No one had heard her speak a bad word about him, but some did wonder why she had so abruptly stopped attending church services many years ago. She had been such a faithful member until then.

Some speculated whether Bagston's untimely death was an accident or not. Seems the halo he wore, in the eyes of many, had sprouted horns in the eyes of others. Had someone done the unthinkable? Millie couldn't even entertain such a thought. The whole ugly mess had only added to the distress in Millie's mind, and she felt like she was about to blow. She knew talking to her family was out of the question. Seeking solace with any of the Baptist congregation was also unthinkable. That could open up more than she was willing to share, more than she could let herself deal with now.

Papa had sent Millie to the only place he could get his favorite tobacco. That was where Florence was finishing up the day's shift. Millie approached her with her heart pounding so loud she was sure anyone could hear. Florence, or Miss Flo as Millie called her, was a kindly woman and older than Millie by years that she was too polite to mention.

As Millie got closer, Miss Flo could see that Millie was greatly troubled. "Can I help you?"

"Papa wants his chewing tobacco," said Millie.

"Well, it's right here on the shelf where it's always been." Flo wondered what had Millie in such a state.

"Millie, you seem to have other things on your mind today. Is everything alright at home? Your Mama's not sick again, is she?"

Millie dropped her head, afraid that everything she was thinking was flashing on her face like some kind of neon sign. "No M'aam, Mama's fine. Thanks for asking." Millie wished she could just disappear, but before she knew it she heard a voice saying, "Could you and I have a cup of coffee together sometime and just talk?" She realized it was her voice speaking up so boldly. Maybe Miss Flo had not heard her.

"Why, of course we can, Millie. Anytime you want to." There was no taking back the words now. Millie hurriedly picked up what she came for, paid for it and took off out the door before she embarrassed herself more.

Coffee Shop Outlaws

The Downtown Coffee Shop still did a lot of business, even though a new Starbucks had opened out by the mall. Generations of folks had been meeting there, saying hello, catching up, mulling over the local situation and the state of the nation, while drinking an unending supply of coffee, Co' Cola, and sweet iced tea.

Luther and Charley sat at a back table.

"How come you're not a Christian?" asked Charley. "You seem to have most everything else in place."

"Well, Charley, you know I could ask how come you're not a Republican? Don't you think there is some kind of implication behind a question like that?"

"Luther, you know those questions aren't the same! Whether I'm a Republican or not won't affect the eternal state of my soul!"

"Not according to some Democrats!" laughed Luther.

"No, seriously. Why aren't you a Christian? You're a smart man."

"Charley, if it makes you feel any better, I **am** a Jesusian. (He pronounced it Gee-Soos-Ee-Uhn). I love Jesus and I follow his teachings. I know, you want to know why I don't go to church and do all the other things your Baptist community says the Bible says to do."

Luther continued. "I don't want to butt heads with you on this, Charley. I love you like a brother. So for now, let's just say we belong to different thought communities."

"What do you mean?"

"How many people are there on earth today, Charley? Several billion? Well, each one is born into a thought community. The family a person is born into has a set of beliefs and customs and habits and understandings that reflect the community around them. Everybody in this thought community rarely questions this set of understandings of THE WAY THINGS REALLY ARE and thinks that people in other thought communities are poor misguided souls. Make sense?"

"Yes, Luther. But my thought community really does have the truth."

"There you go," said Luther.

There was a lull in their conversation as Charley sat adjusting his vision to Luther's point of view. He truly wanted to understand Luther's thinking.

Charley said, "Did you know that coffee shops have been outlawed from time to time by governments in various cultures?"

Luther grinned, "I know you well enough now, Charley, to know what you are doing. Rather than respond directly to what I just said, you are going what seems to be way off somewhere else, then coming in, while my attention is diverted, for the kill."

They both laughed. "No, I'm sincere, Luther. Folk would get together and drink coffee, get all jazzed up, and all kinds of ideas would come pouring out. Some of them would be ideas the government didn't like, regarded as a threat."

"Kind of like what we are doing now?"

"Yep. We are a potential threat to the establishment, any establishment, any predetermined set of ideas that are held to be true and rigidly enforced."

"You mean like religion?"

"Well, Luther, I'm glad you brought that up."

"O Lord, I've done it now, played right into your hands."

"Interesting you should call on the Lord, Luther. You're going to need all the help you can get."

"Okay, lay it on me. I'm listening."

"What you said about thought communities is true and real, but only up to a certain point. It's just part of the picture. What you said is reasonable, but God... I know, I know. You have trouble with that word. Put your own word in there: Origin, Wellspring, Source, Great Mystery. But I'm going to keep saying God. It's a fine word to me."

"Where was I? What you said is reasonable, but God goes far beyond reason. God is Love, Luther. So even though we are all encased in our thought structures and either cannot or refuse to go beyond them, when we move into the realm of Love all of that disappears."

Luther threw his hands up in the air in mock despair. "What am I going to do with you, Charley? Every time I try to be Reasonable, you get all Loving on me. And I warn you, you better stay on your side of the table!"

The two friends laughed. And with that laughter, all differences disappeared.

Spiritual Criminology

Viola was a spiritual counselor but regarded herself as a criminologist.

In her talks on spiritual criminology she would give invited addresses at the local junior college (one of her friends taught Criminal Justice courses and took the class to the "outer limits," as he called it, by inviting her in to speak; another taught Introduction to Theology, where as guest speaker, Viola would emphasize "crimes against God.").

Viola was also in demand as a speaker at many of the local churches.

Viola's thinking of herself as a spiritual criminologist came from her father being a detective, a very good one, with the Atlanta Police Department.

As a child, she had gone with her father to his job on one of those bring-your-kid-to-work days and had been hooked on crime-solving ever since. Her father saw her natural interest and tutored her throughout her childhood and adolescence in solving problems from sketchy information.

But Viola's true calling was counseling. She could see into the depths of people quickly and quietly. Her manner was nonthreatening yet sharply discerning.

In the little town in which she practiced her profession, drawing clientele as well from the surrounding county, she saw many wounded souls.

"A crime," she would say in her talks, "is a violation. There are crimes against property, the violation of property bounds. There are crimes against persons, violations of a person's body. There are crimes against a person's spirit and very soul. I regard spiritual violations as the worst crimes of all."

As a spiritual counselor, Viola was well aware that the culprit, the offender was usually no longer "out there," but had become part of the victim's own being. The person sitting before her was composed of those two parts: the internalized offender and the suffering victim.

Viola's job was to assist the person in resolving this deadly dance.

Viola's Interview

"...and this is Buzz Forman, delight of all women and role model for those of the masculine persuasion! This is your rack-em-up, rouse-em-up, let-er-buck fave-o-rite radio hookup, WYRU, always asking that eternal question, why are you anyway? And to give us some insight on this, we switch out of our studio here to the woman who knows how to let the holy roll, our religion correspondent, that righteous babe, Samantha Tubbs! Sammy doll, what do you have for us today?"

"Buzz, I see you continue to be one of the faithful. You are as faithfully offensive as ever! All that love back atcha! Today we have with us Viola Trumpett, a practicing spiritual criminologist. Good morning, Viola."

"Good morning, Samantha. Is Buzz always like that?"

"Don't let him get to you, dear. That's his shtick, his radio thing he does. He's actually a shy neurotic geeky nerd who lives off an allowance from his daddy. Don't look so shocked, Vi ! I'm just enjoying a little payback time. Giving the devil his due, so to speak. Is that a spiritual crime? What is a spiritual criminologist anyway? I never heard of one before. Is that a criminologist who is spiritual?"

Viola laughs. "Not necessarily. It's a criminologist who specializes in spiritual crimes."

Samantha speaks in puzzled tones. "I don't get it. You mean like robbing a church instead of a liquor store?"

"No. I mean crimes against the spirit; actions and stances that wound the very soul."

"You mean like hurt somebody's feelings?"

"Yes, but as an offense, that would be analogous to jay-walking, going against and cutting across another person's emotional traffic. That would be more like a misdemeanor, your demeanor is misappropriate. Some folk adopt an offensive demeanor as their way of life."

"Uh-oh. You mean like Buzz and me. But if we don't really hurt each other's feelings, that's okay, isn't it? It's not a spiritual crime?"

"Not in a hard-core sense, no. But you have to consider what you are bringing into the world. You are helping create a sarcastic cynical tone in life's music."

"Gee, Viola! Can't we play and have fun!?"

Viola laughs. "Of course, Samantha! Laughter and spiritual health are intertwined."

"Whew! I thought you were about to go all religious on us."

"That's interesting. People often confuse religion with spirituality. I am not a religious criminologist. I am a spiritual criminologist."

"Let's hold it right there for a message from our sponsor of this segment – the Maddox-Huxley Funeral Home serving Chattahoochee County since 1912." Samantha plays a pre-recorded ad asking folk to consider Maddox-Huxley as "the place of preparation for entering the Great Beyond."

"Okay. We're back. This morning we have with us Viola Trumpett, spiritual criminologist. An interesting conversation, thus far. Viola, what does a spiritual criminologist actually do?"

"First of all, Samantha, I need to tell you what a spiritual crime is. I think I haven't made that clear. A crime is a violation. There are crimes against property, the violation of property bounds. There are crimes against persons, violations of a person's body. There are crimes against a person's spirit and very soul. These are spiritual violations, violations which I regard as the worst crimes of all. When a person's spirit is warped or diminished, that is infinitely worse than the stealing of property or doing physical harm."

Samantha (recalling some of her own experiences): "I am beginning to see what you mean."

"A spiritual criminologist then is attuned to the detecting and resolving of spiritual crimes. In doing so, she or he works with the professionals in other realms – law enforcement; the staff of churches, temples, and synagogues; psychology; psychiatry, the military, and so on."

"What do you mean by detecting? You mean like a detective, like Sherlock Holmes?"

"Yes, like that. One has to go to where the crime has taken place. With one difference. Not only does the spiritual criminologist investigate the external environs for clues and understandings, but also and perhaps even more importantly the internal environs, the person's very soul."

"Wow, Viola. I'm amazed. How does a person get the training for such a challenging profession? It doesn't sound like it's something a mere mortal can do."

"Yes, one needs training, extensive training and practice under the tutelage of someone who knows what they are doing. But the basic skills we all have and use, especially with our friends. We can often intuit what is wrong, how and why someone is suffering. And we can often help them resolve it. Each one of us practices to some extent as amateur spiritual criminologists."

"Thank you, Viola! That is all the time we have today. Thank you for being with us!"

"You are welcome, Samantha. Thank you."

"And now a word from our sponsor for the segment of our show you just heard – Wiggly's Dog Biscuits, the chow that makes your dog bow-wow!"

Jungle Gyms of the Mind

Charley appreciated what Luther had said about thought communities. It wasn't that he hadn't thought about this before.

His take on thought structures and belief systems was that they were like the jungle gyms, those steel-barred open structures in the shape of half a sphere, that used to grace school playgrounds until child endangerment ("all children will have to wear safety helmets while swinging on the jungle gym") and threat of lawsuits ("no child can play on the jungle gym without parental written permission") hastened their extinction.

A belief system, thought Charley, *provides the same service as a jungle gym – a lot of creative opportunity for daring movements that exercise the heart, mind, and soul. Without a belief system to swing around in, where would you be?*

Charley was aware that the Baptists were folk who rejected earlier belief systems as too cramping, too small, too restrictive for their spiritual tastes.

He had begun feeling the same way about what Brother Bagston was teaching and preaching before his untimely and energetic demise. *Why the man had practically hurled his head toward an unforgiving communion table!* Bagston's theological jungle gym was too restrictive, too small.

Charley had started looking at the teachings and actions of Jesus while setting aside all the church stuff that had grown up around him. The results were startling.

Charley was seeing things in a new and different light now than the so-called hardshell Baptists – the mossybacks he sometimes called them.

But Charley was smart enough to realize that he too was still caught up in a belief system. He was beginning to give more attention to a verse in Philippians about Jesus emptying himself. He was learning more about this from the Christian mystics, especially Meister Eckhart and John Ruysbroeck, who had a lot to say in favor of letting go into God, beyond all human structure.

Another concern of Charley's was Millie Huckleberry. He knew she carried a ton of internal baggage. He knew Millie was a good person, but something, probably more than one thing, was eating at her. He had noticed that Millie thought highly of Flo, or "Miss Flo" as Millie called her.

Charley hoped that Millie would confide in Miss Flo, beginning the process of allowing someone to see her woundings.

Thelma's Right Boob

Thelma bit another chunk out of her Moon Pie and washed it down with another slug of her R C Cola. "That little slut!" she said aloud.

"What's the matter with you now, honey?" asked Junior a little fearfully. As her husband of many years (they had dated since high school), he knew to get ready to duck if she got riled.

"Oh, that little slut Millie! I don't know why ever body cain't see right thoo her." Crumbs of Moon Pie clung precariously to the corners of her mouth. Junior watched them with interest as she talked, wondering which corner would fall first onto his wife's ample bosom.

"She led Brother Bagston along with her hussy ways, acting all pure and all. That pore man didn't have a chance, the way she wiggled her hips and flounced herself at him."

"Why Thelma! I don't think Millie is that way at all!"

"Hush your mouth, Junior! You are just like all men, easily taken in by a woman's wiles."

"Yeah, like yours for instance," Junior muttered, thinking that when they first got together, Thelma would do about anything Junior would want in bed, but that changed quickly after their wedding vows were spoken.

"What did you say, Junior?!" The right crumb won, bouncing off the ski slope of Thelma's right boob and landing on the floor where it was immediately gobbled up by their Irish Setter, Blaze.

"Nothing, honey," he said, falling back into the state of semi-stupor he had adopted thinking a trance state was the husbandly and Christian thing to do to keep the peace.

"Well, I think she had a hand in Bagston's death and I hope the little tart gets what's coming to her!"

A Twenty In His Nostril

The lines of powder lay there, reflected in the mirror like miniature snowy landscapes reflected in a lake. Her husband looked odd, almost comical, standing there with the rolled-up twenty stuck in his nostril.

She had walked in unexpectedly. He was startled.

Suddenly things fell into place for her, things that earlier made no sense. She just thought it was maybe part of a midlife crisis or some problem at the church bothering him– his mood swings, lethargic one moment and then quickly up and running, his grinding of his teeth, his increased irritation.

She knew what she was looking at. She had heard about this on Oprah and on Dr. Phil.

Her husband, the Right Reverend Melvin T. Bagston, was a cocaine addict.

Brother Ted

A mainstay of the church, and Charley's mentor, was old Brother Wilson. Ted Wilson was a walking embodiment of the teachings of Jesus, a humble man who could see others quite clearly, both their good and their ornery. He was a loving man who had gone through more than one well-marked Bible and had views that most were too busy to hear, not that Ted Wilson looked to enforce his views on anyone.

But Charley wanted to hear, and he and Brother Ted had many conversations. With Brother Ted, Charley felt accepted, understood, appreciated as he was. A rare commodity in this day's world.

Ted's mind ranged out in many directions, while keeping his beloved Jesus central to his understandings and at the core of his heart. It was Ted that introduced Charley to the mystics, first the Christian mystics, then the mystics of other religions and cultures.

It was Ted who helped Charley see more deeply that not only folk of other Christian faiths had a close relationship with God, but also folk of other religions and other cultures. To the orthodox Baptist, this was unthinkable heresy. How could God be in the lives of anyone who did not have Jesus as their Personal Savior?

Most folks did not seem too concerned about these matters. And Charley and Ted understood that. That was fine. Folk were busy living their lives and never thought to raise questions of that sort.

Charley and Ted loved their little church and sometimes wondered what Jesus would say if he walked in one day in a suit and a haircut and gave the invited sermon.

Ted thought that Jesus wouldn't have to say much. Some would be running out the door. Others would be crying, laughing, and happy.

Ted's words were prophetic. But it wouldn't be Jesus giving the sermon, it would be one of his representatives.

The Light

The Light that lit people's hearts waited quietly.

People were forever obscuring themselves, clouding themselves with things-to-do, with emotions, with self-reflections, with Dr. Phil, with anything they could find.

People seemed to have lost the art of sitting quietly and making room in the In.

No. It wasn't that they had lost the art. They simply didn't want to.

The Light sighed, sending out a brilliant flow of warmth and wisdom, which no one received.

The Light understood. Humans were made of dirt, water, air, and fire.

The first two were not all that conducive to Light.

The second two transformed it and embodied it as Energy.

The Light understood.

What was needed was capacity, capacity to receive the Light.

And that was up to each human.

Making room, clearing themselves of all the imaginings and goings on and yikkety-yak in their heads. Settling down. Opening up.

The Light was more than willing to come in.

Folk were too busy with their melodramas, too full of themselves to allow it.

What was needed was a healing, a making whole and holy.

And for that people had to make room.

The Light that lit people's hearts waited quietly.

Millie and Miss Flo Meet

Things had settled down some in the town and in the church about the horrific death of their Baptist preacher. If anyone thought this was going to go away, they were mighty wrong. There was a growing rumor that his death was not so accidental. Some of the good church folk refused to see it this way and believed it was just an act of the Good Lord. After all, everyone had a time to go.

Millie had found no quenching of the fire she carried inside her. She gathered up all the courage she could and bravely marched herself into the 5 and 10, right up to Miss Flo. "Would you like to have that cup of coffee today? I really need somebody to talk to."

Millie's request was so urgent that it startled Miss Flo, not to mention several of the customers nearby.

"Can you wait until my lunch break, Millie?" Flo could see the storm inside Millie and wanted to help.

"Yes, can we meet at the coffee shop around noon?" They both agreed. There was no going back now for Millie. She didn't know how she was going to hold it all in that long, but it would give her time to calm down a mite and not scare away the only person she felt she could confide in.

Millie got to the coffee shop early so she could choose a table in the back corner that would give some sort of privacy. What was she thinking to suggest the one place that most of the townsfolk frequented? And at lunchtime too? Well, it would just have to do for the first of many meetings Millie hoped to have with someone she felt she could trust.

Right on time, Miss Flo arrived and came straight to where Millie was sitting. "Millie, you sounded so urgent. Are you alright?"

"Yes, Ma'am. I just need someone to talk to."

"Well, I'm glad you chose me, Millie. I want you to know whatever you tell me will be kept strictly between us."

"Miss Flo, I don't know where to start."

"Well, Millie, just take a deep breath and start wherever you want to."

"Have you ever felt different?" Millie asked. "I mean really different, as if you don't belong anywhere?"

"I think everyone has felt that at some time, Millie."

"Well, I feel that all the time. I don't fit in at home, or at church. I listen to what some folks say they feel and believe at church, but they don't always seem to live it. Now, I know everyone at church can't be like this. Take Miss Jeanine, the ladies Sunday School teacher, she lives what she teaches. (In this small Southern town, all women of older years were called "Miss" as a matter of respect. It didn't matter whether they were married or not.) I just don't know what to believe anymore. And I don't think I can tell you how I feel about Bro. Bagston."

"Did he hurt you in some way, Millie?" Miss Flo had a tone in her voice that Millie had never heard before.

"No, I just don't understand why someone who calls himself a man of God can do some of the things he did. You know I did some work over at the church for awhile."

"Yes, I heard about that. The ladies that come in the store do love to talk. Do you know something about Bagston that you can tell me?"

Millie took a deep breath and let it spill out, "I heard arguments between him and the head of deacons. It was about some church bonds. The deacon was mighty mad." She was on a roll now and it couldn't be stopped. "And I didn't like the way he acted around me, either. It made me feel kinda important at first, but then it got creepy. I've never had a man act that way around me before."

"Miss Flo, I feel sort of funny speaking so unkindly about the dead. I think God's gonna be upset with me."

"Nothing of the sort," Flo answered. "God knows you better than anyone else. He loves you, and he knows what a good heart you have."

"You speak so well of God, but you don't go to church." Millie was ashamed of what she had just said. It sounded like some of the judgmental talk she had heard from others.

"I have my reasons for not attending church, but I do believe in God. I still read my Bible and pray."

"Miss Flo, there is so much else I want to ask you about. Like when I….." Millie was stopped in mid sentence by Charley coming over to their table to say a polite hello.

Charley knew he was interrupting something as he got closer to the table, but it was too late now. He got out of the awkwardness as gracefully as possible.

"Hello, Flo. Millie. Just wanted to say hi, that's all. So blessings to you. Got to be on my way! Have a good lunch." And with that he turned and walked away.

"So what were you saying, Millie?" asked a concerned Flo.

"Gosh, Miss Flo. I feel like I have already said too much. You must think I'm crazy."

"No. I don't. Please go on, Millie."

"Well, some folks say that Bro. Bagston's death was not an accident. I kinda believe them. I don't know who might have done it, but I just have a strong feeling someone did."

Flo seemed troubled for a moment over Millie's words. Finally, she said, "Well, he wasn't a very nice person, even though he was a preacher. So many people go around acting like they are living in the Light, but are in total darkness and danger of losing their immortal souls. I fear you have been influenced by some of these people."

"Yes, you are right." Millie could think of those in the church who seemed so pious. She believed what they told her even though it sounded strange to her at times. After all, they said it with confidence. Millie didn't know that some people will say anything to make themselves look big. What she had been doing was looking to others for her salvation and not to the Light, God's Son.

Flo realized that her lunchtime was over and she had to get back to work. "Millie, can we please get together again soon? I so appreciate your opening up to me and sharing so much."

"Yes, Miss Flo. Whenever you can." They clasped hands and shared a knowing smile with each other before Flo turned and left.

Charley had to be on his way to make the hospital visits now that Bro. Bagston was gone. The deacons had elected Charley as interim pastor until a permanent one could be found. But he would make time to go over and speak to Millie again now that she was alone. Millie had always caught his eye, but he was never able to bring himself to pursue her. She always seemed so shy and preoccupied.

"Millie, may I sit down a minute? We rarely have a chance to talk."

Millie was glad to have his company for awhile and asked him to sit.

"I am glad to see you spending time with Flo. She can be a good friend."

"Well, we are not exactly friends, yet. But I just know she is someone I can trust." Millie didn't want to let on that she had just poured out her heart to Miss Flo. And she could hardly wait to confide in her again.

Charley was not a shy person, but when he was in the presence of Millie he could hardly get his words out. "I'd like for us to be friends, Millie."

"I'd like that too, Charley. But I have to go now. Papa is expecting me at home."

They said their good-byes and Charley watched Millie walk away, wondering if he could ever tell her how he really felt.

Two Horny Dudes

He watched the old broad leave.

The cute young one, definitely well within the range for breeding, stayed behind, toying with her napkin and looking to be in some sort of trance state. *Thinking*, the humans called it, *this losing awareness of what was around them*. And that could be dangerous. Especially if he or his cronies were around.

Hmmm…. She was a nice little package. He could feel his flaccid horns begin to pulse with blood beneath his hat. He chuckled. If only humans understood what being horny really meant.

Ha! Here came that little mealy-mouthed preacher dude. Just as horny as he was, but instead turned that excess blood flow into shuffling embarrassment. *What a loser! It was obvious he had an in with the girl, but he didn't know how to cut himself a slice of that pie. Probably wouldn't know what to do with it if he did.*

He laughed at his metaphor. He was learning this American language purty doggone good!

She left and walked right by him, totally unaware in her sweet sweetness of his existence. *Good! All the better for when the time came.*

The preacher dude noticed him though. Noticed him noticing her. He may not have horns but the little bozo definitely had antennae!

Gregor paid his bill and left.

Jeanine

Jeanine Bulloch had been the women's Sunday School teacher for many years. She was an outgoing lady and sometimes misunderstood because of her frankness. As the older folks said, "She calls 'em as she sees 'em." Jeanine was a staunch believer in the Baptist Faith and Doctrine not because God or heaven was exclusively for the Baptists, but she believed in the Word of God, the Bible, as the absolute truth. No one had ever accused Jeanine of being a Pharisee. You know, one of those "religious" people who had such difficulty with Jesus' teachings. Jeanine didn't have much use for this sort. She had seen too many people hurt by them.

The ladies in Jeanine's class were regular in attendance. There were some pretty important discussions going on there. It was a place where they were free to express their opinions or ask any question without being judged. Sometimes they came full of life's problems and were able to share with the class, leaving them with relief of soul when they left. Tears and laughter were commonplace.

Some had a problem with the Baptist quarterly not being strictly followed in the class. But Jeanine knew that folks sometimes had to be ministered to in their present circumstances. Jesus did this during His earthly ministry.

Millie and Viola were members of this class. Though Millie had never been able to share much of her inner self, she enjoyed very much being with others who could. Viola had no difficulty at all.

What Jeanine tried to convey to her class was to seek a relationship with God that required them spending time with God in prayer and in His Word. Most folks never caught on to that. They had too much going on in their lives to have time for this. Except when they were in trouble or needed something. Then, they had no problem asking. For some this was done as a public show at the altar on Sunday morning. They did not get God's attention as much as they did the congregation's.

The Angel of Fire

The Angel of Fire, like all beings, including human ones, could not remember when he did not exist. For certain, he was present at the time of the Burning Bush and the barefoot Moses, and definitely when that complaining and bedraggled band of exiles that Moses led went staggering around the desert following the Pillar.

He also recalled the extraordinary surging of power and energy when he came flashing down from the heavens and helped Elijah make fools out of those self-proclaimed sorcerers.

Elijah! Now there was a man! Elijah lived with the Elementals, surfed on the waves of Eternal Energy, lived at the edge and circumference of It All. Elijah didn't try to just make do and get through the day. Elijah Dared!

Ah well, sighed the Angel. *Humans were in another era now, had tamed themselves to fit in job slots, had willingly clipped their own wings in their search for security.* His job of the moment was to help raise their consciousness another notch, to help open understandings and awareness to the Cosmocracy in which they really lived. And they needed Fire to do that!

He was ready to put some Zing in their heart, some Pizazz in their walk, some Spiz-uh-muh-ri-gum at the very base of their souls!

He saw already that some of the residents of this little town would understand immediately when he approached them. Some of the others had quite a surprise coming their way!

The Angel of Fire chuckled as he began the process of Transmutation into human form.

The true essence of the elderly man he became could be recognized only by his flashing eyes.

Millie's Walk Home

Millie hurried on her way home, so as not to make Papa mad. Papa got mad a lot. Millie was used to his occasional drinking and how loud he got when he was in what Mama called his "tipsy way." When he was like this he wasn't mad at any particular person. Just at the world in general. But Millie couldn't handle it when Papa got mad at her. Though she rarely gave him occasion. Confrontation was not one of Millie's strong suits.

The talk with Miss Flo gave Millie a feeling she had never had before. She wouldn't have known how to describe it if someone had asked her. It was a kind of joy and freedom. Made her feel like skipping all the way home. She hadn't done that since she was a little girl. It was hard for her to believe how easy the words came as she told Miss Flo of her deepest secrets. Miss Flo didn't have a bad reaction at all. She listened to Millie as if she had good sense.

Maybe it wouldn't be so hard for Millie to talk to others now. Not just anybody, of course. But Miss Jeanine was certainly a person she had in mind. Now wouldn't that be something if Millie could take part in the conversations in Sunday School? Maybe they would laugh at her, and maybe not. All the other ladies didn't seem to have a problem bearing their souls. And no one had laughed at them. Anyway, she would just stick to opening up to Miss Flo right now. But who knows?

She had certainly not forgotten the attention Charley paid to her at the coffee shop. He was a handsome young man. But Millie was sure he just felt sorry for her. Guess he was just practicing his "preacher ways" on her.

Sunday Afternoon in the Park

The next meeting with Miss Flo couldn't come soon enough for Millie. All the feelings she had stuffed down inside were now swimming on the surface. She was fairly close to bursting.

She and Flo had decided they would spend a Sunday afternoon together. Millie was to meet her at the park. She was afraid when she saw Miss Flo that she would knock her down with the storm of emotions and thoughts she had bottled up so long. As she walked to the park, she practiced what she would say. But she knew it was no use. Nothing could stop her now.

As they sat on a bench under one of the biggest shade trees in the town's little park, Millie began to talk as naturally as if she had done it all her life. So this was what it was like to have a friend, one you could share with. It made Millie feel as if she was in her own "tipsy way."

Time passed unnoticed as they chattered away. Even the dark, scary things Millie hated so much to talk about didn't seem so overwhelming any more. She talked about Papa, Mama, Bro. Bagston, and even what some of the townsfolk were saying about her. Millie had heard rumors about her and Bagston being at the church alone. She couldn't imagine what caused people to say such things. Mama would say their minds needed a good washing.

Millie learned some things about Miss Flo that day. She saw hurt in the eyes of her new friend when they talked about Bro. Bagston and gossipy town folk. Why had she never noticed before that Miss Flo might have dark secrets of her own? Some things that caused her pain. Millie had never brought herself to really look people in the eyes. She thought them all above her. Only she could have those kind of feelings. Well, today she found out how wrong she was.

Atlanta

"Freddy, go down there."

"Want me to take anyone with me?"

"No, we'll play it quietly for a while. Scope it out, Freddy."

"It's just like that horse's ass Bagston to stumble over his own feet and kill his self."

"Yeah, seems that way, doesn't it? I'm happy not to have to deal with him anymore. What a sanctimonious prig! But I don't think he killed himself taking that dive."

"You think somebody offed him?"

"That was a pretty quick cremation. No autopsy could be performed if ever called for. Besides, the Baptists in general don't take to cremation. They go for full body burial."

"That rise again thing, huh?"

"Whatever. Go down there, Freddy. Keep a low profile. Snoop around. See what you can find."

"On my way!"

"And, Freddy, keep an eye out for someone in that little church that could take Bagston's place in cutting us a deal."

The Boys Play

Charley threw a haymaker at Luther's chin with full force.

Luther spun, stepping inside and blending with Charley's onrushing energy, and effortlessly threw him to the ground. Luther followed up with a barely withheld but ferocious kick heel-first to Charley's sternum.

Charley lay there getting his breath.

"Luther, that kick while I was down wasn't a very Christian thing to do!"

"Charley, you forget. I don't consider myself a Christian." He helped Charley up. "Besides, doesn't it say in your Holy Book that if your eye offends you, you are to pluck it out?"

"I don't think it means to kick me while I'm down!"

"Charley! Fighting is exactly that! Fighting! If you are not going to disable your opponent, then you are just playing some sort of dangerous game."

"But...."

"No buts. Have you ever seen one of those movies where a person holds a gun on the bad guy but keeps talking to him, until finally the bad guy takes the gun away?"

"Well, yeah."

"If you are going to pull a gun, you better use it. At least pop one in their knee cap. Otherwise, don't pull a gun at all. The other person will quickly know you don't intend to use it. Then your butt is in for a world of hurt."

"I just don't think that way, Luther."

"I know you don't, Charley. You are not a gun or knife man. You have pretty good instincts at hand-to-hand combat though!" Without warning of any kind, Luther aimed a kick at Charley.

Charley caught the kick with a scooping block, then swept Luther's supporting leg from under him.

They both laughed.

"See what I mean, Charley? You are, underneath it all, one fierce dude!"

Millie The Librarian

Millie had found that spending time away from home while working at the church had made her feel useful. When she heard of a part-time job open at the public library she grabbed it. As she was on her way to work one afternoon she ran over in her mind the uneasy feelings she had about Bro. Bagston's peculiar death. Why did Mrs. Bagston have him cremated in such a hurry? After all, the church did not believe in cremation. And the good wife of our dead preacher would never go against the teachings of the church. It would mar her standing in the community. That's something she would never jeopardize. She had offered no explanation, but then she was not used to having to give an explanation of her conduct to anyone. She sure seemed mighty cheerful for someone who had just lost her husband. Maybe she was just putting on a brave face. This was something she would surely have to discuss with Viola. Her experience with the law and crime matters could put Millie's mind to rest on this subject.

As she walked in the warm sun, Millie felt free as a bird. You hear about prisoners sitting in a jail cell with the door open and refusing to leave because they had gotten used to their imprisonment. Not Millie. When those prison bars opened for her, she came running out! And there was no turning back. Out she was, and out she would stay.

Millie had spent many hours in the company of Miss Flo. They talked like two school girls at a spend-the-night party. Why Millie had even shared her intentions towards Charley. Poor Charley. Two women scheming against him.

Ted and Charley

Ted and Charley sat on a bench in the shade of a tree on the town square. A soft breeze blew. Horns honked and folk they knew waved as they drove by.

The older man and Charley sat quietly. Charley knew that Ted would not just leap into a conversation like most folk, but liked to sit for a while to see what would emerge. Charley had grown comfortable with sitting in the silence.

After a while, Ted said, "Charley, if you could see sound as well as hear it, how could you tell others your experience?"

"Why, I would just come right out and say it!"

"Would they believe you?"

Charley sat for a while, running the reactions of folk he knew through his mind. "No."

"What would be their reaction, Charley?"

"Some would look at you like you were crazy. Others would say, 'Oh, that's just Charley again.' Many wouldn't even give it a thought, wouldn't even really hear what I was saying."

They sat silently for a while.

"Why wouldn't they hear what you are saying, Charley? Why wouldn't they be interested and want to know how a person could do that? Why wouldn't they want to learn to do it themselves?"

Charley thought for a while.

"Too much trouble. Folk want to just go along with the way of thinking they have been taught. They have made a comfortable life with that." He paused. "Besides, it might mess up their standing in the community, believing such stuff. Around here, you have to believe what everybody else believes or you are a goner."

Church bells sounded the time.

"And Charley, what if they met every week and affirmed to each other that sound could only be heard and never seen and you were a member of the group but you knew differently?"

"You wouldn't have many options, Brother Ted. You'd have to keep your mouth shut, try to tell the others, or leave."

They sat quietly together for quite a while.

Jesus In the Forest

After their martial arts workout, Luther and Charley sauntered in to the Downtown Coffee Shop for a cold fruit Smoothie.

Luther said, "Charley, did you hear about the Baptist that met Jesus in the woods?"

"Luther, I don't want to hear any Jesus jokes."

"No, Charley. This is a story, kind of a parable. Ted told it to me."

"Well, if Ted told it to you, I want to hear it."

Their Smoothies came and they took a moment, inhaling the icy fruit blend until their throats ached with cold.

"This man was walking through the woods full of zeal and fervor,...."

"Full of zeal and fervor? Where did you get those words, Luther?"

"Don't give me grief, Charley! Just shut up and listen. I told you Ted told me this. Alright! The guy was all pumped! Okay?"

They both laughed.

"So this man was walking through the woods all full of zeal and fervor, all pumped, and he saw Jesus walking toward him. Only he didn't know it was Jesus."

He paused for some more Smoothie.

"So he starts witnessing to Jesus and concludes by saying to Jesus, 'And sir, if you don't believe as I believe and see things as I see them, you are going to Hell.'"

"Jesus looked at him with those loving and compassionate, yet fierce, eyes and says, "Sir, if you don't see things as I see them, you are in Hell already!'"

Their straws signaled they had bottomed out on their liquid refreshments.

"What sense do you make of that, Luther?"

"Christ consciousness, Charley! Christ consciousness! It's not about beliefs and hell and heaven! It's about having the mind of Christ. Here! Right now!"

"Luther, you amaze me. Sometimes you make a lot of sense.

Viola

Viola was accustomed to people telling about themselves and their situations. Speaking from their own point of view. Their own viewing point. A point no one else could occupy. Oh, someone else might stand as close to that point as possible. But everyone occupied their own point. And everyone thought their point of view was reality.

And it was, of course. But only one reality out of billions (ever how many people on earth, how many were there now?, everybody breeding like rabbits, she thought) of points of view.

It's amazing we can communicate with each other at all, she mused. Of course it helps that people think they are in the same reality and don't even question that they are not.

Viola knew better. She became especially quiet and still when others spoke, rid herself of her self, her mind chatter, her views about the-way-things-should-be. She knew better than to try to give advice. Disastrous! That never went anywhere except down the drain.

Emptying herself of self, as it was said that Jesus did in the Holy Book, she allowed her awareness, her energies to merge with whoever sat before her. Her consciousness, her awareness moved right along with theirs. Wherever they went, Viola moved with them.

Sometimes, with the things she was told, the only link to her sanity was her practice of deep centering, anchoring, and grounding. She moved with others while remaining immovable at her core.

It was fortunate she had such lengthy practice. She was about to receive a visitor who would push her skills to the limit and leave her shaken to her depths.

Freddy and Gregor were about to keep an appointment.

Viola and the I Ching

After the man who identified himself as Freddy Tempest had called and said he wanted to come in and talk over some things that had been bothering him, and oh! he wanted to bring his partner Gregor, who could cast some light on these "issues," Viola heard familiar alarm bells sounding off in her soul.

Issues!, she thought. She wished that word had never entered the popular realm of psychobabble. Now everyone and her sister were having issues! She remembered laughing with her counseling buddies: "Here come the issues! Stock up on the tissues!" and, even worse, falling into punning, wondering why people didn't have more health issue-ance. Ah well, every profession dealing with people had its gallows humor. It was one way of surviving the constant onslaught of trauma and pain.

But there was something disturbing about that phone call and its intent.

Though firmly ensconced in a Baptist community, Viola respected the wisdom of other cultures. In Vedanta language, she regarded Jesus as her Root Guru, though she would say it that way in the presence of only a few others, Ted for example.

Her decision long ago to not attend a Baptist seminary, but to attend a "secular" university resulted in her becoming acquainted with the I Ching, the Chinese Book of Changes. It had come up in a course on "Shamanism and Entheogenics" and her becoming fascinated with a book on the reading list, Terence and Dennis McKenna's *The Invisible Landscape*. She had been casting the I Ching at appropriate times ever since, always finding it right on the mark in its responses.

Now seemed like one of those appropriate times.

She moved into her intuitional mode where she felt in resonance and harmony and followed the 2800 year old procedure. She used the coin method instead of yarrow sticks. While tossing the coins, she allowed images to arise of the community and its people she loved so dearly, of the little Baptist church and its lovely grounds, of the phone call she had received, and of the two men coming in to see her.

28. Ta Kuo / Preponderance of the Great with a moving line in the sixth place.

She read the text. "The load is too heavy for the strength of the supports. The ridgepole, on which the whole roof rests, sags to the breaking point, because its supporting ends are too weak for the load they bear. It is an exceptional time and situation; therefore extraordinary measures are demanded. It is necessary to find a way of transition as quickly as possible, and to take action. This promises success."

She sighed. She knew since Bagston's death and the rumors of his involving the church in some highly questionable financial transactions, that the I Ching was pointing in that direction.

Viola turned to the sixth line, the only line that was moving, knowing that whatever it said was especially related to her. She read it with alarm, then with strong resignation and commitment.

"One must go through the water. It goes over one's head. Misfortune. No blame."

The commentary on the line read: "Here is a situation in which the unusual has reached a climax. One is courageous and wishes to accomplish one's task, no matter what happens. This leads into danger. The water rises over one's head. This is the misfortune. But one incurs no blame in giving up one's life that the good and the right may prevail. There are things more important than life."

"Help me, sweet Jesus!" she exclaimed from her depths. She knew she was about to engage in the fight of her life. And possibly, her death.

Encounter

He keeps his hat on indoors. Maybe it has to do with his religion, Viola mused. *His eyes are green. They have a fiery kind of shine when he gets excited.*

As now.

"Miss Trumpett, I meant no harm. I didn't mean to upset you. (two lies in rapid succession.) I , we..." Gregor glanced at his partner Freddy, "just thought that since you were rather new to the community you might be more sympathetic to our point of view."

"Well, Mr. Gregor (was that his first or last name? he only gave the one), I'm not!"

Freddy, who seemed to be playing the good cop role to Gregor's bad, said, "Viola, please excuse my friend. He gets a little excited about this project and tends to get carried away, a little overly enthusiastic."

Viola thought, *Enthusiastic is not the word!* She knew the word's roots came from en-theos (to be filled with the theos, with God's energies). And she did not feel what she felt were God's energies anywhere near Gregor. Quite the opposite. He had a devilish nature.

"Well, Mr. Tempest, you may call it enthusiasm, but I call it abhorrent! What the two of you are really suggesting is that I abandon my code of ethics and become, in essence, a spy for your corporation. Sell my soul, in effect, just so you can build a casino in this town. And destroy a perfectly good church in the process."

Freddy signaled to Gregor to remain quiet and gave it another try.

"We mean no harm. We just wish to bring progress in the form of more jobs and greater income to the community. All it will take is a little development ...."

"You are just digging your hole a little deeper, Mr. Tempest. I have heard those code words before. I know what "progress" and "development" mean to men like you. And as far as income, I know where the money will really go. Not to the community!"

"Well, Viola, we can make sure that it will. I understand you want to build a Wellness Center for the town focusing on the healing of body, mind, and spirit. A worthy endeavor! We can ensure that dream comes true."

"Now it's bribery, is it?" Viola stood up. "This conversation is over. Good bye, gentlemen!"

As the two exited, Gregor turned and gave Viola a look that chilled her to the bone. Though his lips did not move, she heard his rasping voice echo in her mind. *Bitch! You will pay for this!* Despite herself, her anger was undercut by a sudden spasm of fear.

Viola's Peculiar Rambling Prayer

Who does a counselor go to for counseling?

I feel all alone with this shit. Well, there you go, I'm all shook up. When I start cussin' I'm already feeling pushed over the edge.

I already know anyway what advice folk would give me.

Some would look at me with that pious concerned look which is so infuriating and say take it to the Lord in prayer. Others would tell me to go to the police. A few would shake their heads and say it was just my overly vivid imagination. Some would even say take the deal!

Well, I won't be talking with anybody anyway.

She sighed. *Very few people would just LISTEN! Just shut up, get quiet, and listen. Truly hear what I am saying.*

When someone performed that lost and dying art, she could see herself in their quiet mirror, could begin to hear the solutions or next steps to take prompted by her own free-ranging questionings.

She didn't want advice.

She just wanted to be heard.

There was a knock at her heart's door.

The Angel of Fire stood waiting, waiting to be let in.

Gregor Chortles

Gregor chortled, in the way demons do, deep in the throat half-choking and with a sensual thrill.

He was not always a demon. He was once a busynessman.

Not a busynessman in the busyness of serving others, of meeting others' needs by providing a service or helpful product.

Gregor's drive as a busynessman in those days was to make a living by charging as high a price as possible for the least output possible.

He chortled again, this time in the anguished range of nails across a blackboard or someone chewing on aluminum foil, at his naiveté in thinking that anyone could **make** a living. He knew now that living was up to the Maker, not to any human or demon.

At the thought of the Maker, he cringed. Not because of anything to do with the Maker, but with the Unmaker, sometimes called the Under Taker. The first because He was always trying to undo the Maker's work; the second because He was the Boss of the Underworld whose busyness was always taking something from someone, usually from someone who could least afford to have anything taken.

He cringed, because of the shock delivered to him from the dog collar he wore embedded into his neck. It activated anytime Gregor had a thought about the Maker or any thought containing any hint of kindness or truthfulness.

Gregor had naturally linked with the underworld, the gangsters of earthly society. Whether they consciously knew it or not, they were, as he was, in the Unmaker's employ.

Part of Gregor's service to the Unmaker now was to carry out the will of the earthly underworld boss. At the moment (and Gregor's moments stretched into eternity, his contract with the Unmaker had no termination clause), his job was to ensure the demise of the little Baptist church so a casino could be built upon its grounds.

He chortled once again with devilish pleasure at the thought of the souls he would torture and bring down in the process.

Night Visit

"Aha! Two collars meet!" said the green-eyed demon to the priest. His eyes gleamed with mockery, but his voice tone gave a sense of respect, of the meeting of equals, as if they were members of the same club. Or football players on opposing teams.

"I see no collar on you," said the priest.

Gregor showed him the thin flesh-colored collar that had become part of him, as natural to him as the horns lying flat beneath his hair.

"We are brothers of the collar."

"No way. I stand for things you don't!"

"Well, priest, if by "stand" you mean "put up with," you are absolutely right! You put up with a lot of things I would never stand for. People who whine and cry and moan about their lives and want to tell you about it at every opportunity. And you do! You stand for it! Don't you know, haven't you learned by now, that you are rewarding such behavior? You are helping people stay at the level of sniveling idiots rather than stepping up to life and dealing with it head on."

"Uh" ….The priest had had such thoughts himself and didn't know what to say.

"See what I mean? You have had these thoughts yourself."

"That is why I say we are brothers of the collar. I wear the collar of the Unmaker. You wear the collar of the Maker. We each get shocked when we step outside our Boss's bounds. You get a shock when you step into my world, the world of Unmaking. I get a shock when I even think of stepping into yours. We are twins. Mirror images of each other. Admit it! You wouldn't even be in business if it weren't for me and the Unmaker. You'd have to get a respectable job like making doughnuts or driving truck."

The priest did not know what to say, had no comeback. He had often thought of a simpler life than the one he had chosen. No more of the endless round of baptisms and funerals and wedding ceremonies and half-meant confessions and business meetings and …

"Think it over, my brother. I believe we could do a little busyness together. All for the good of the community, too. Folk would no longer take you for granted, but see you as a mover and a shaker."

Gregor kissed him on the lips.

The priest woke from this vivid dream, in his own bed, his lips burning.

Flo's Glock

Flo fired again. She had 13 rounds in her Glock 32. The pistol fired smoothly and evenly. It weighed less than two pounds loaded and its length of less than seven inches made it easily concealed. The .357 magnum bullets it fired gave it strong stopping power (the Glock would punch a bullet through a car door). And Flo had determined if she ever had to use it, whatever was headed toward her would definitely be stopped.

She was an expert shot, producing a tight cluster in the heart of the target every time. One of her brothers had taken her years ago to the countryside to plink some cans with his .22 Ruger single-six. She was good. Soon she had cajoled their parents into giving her a Ruger for her birthday.

Of course she had to go to the appropriate weapons safety program on the base for military dependents (her Dad was in Special Forces), but she enjoyed every minute of it. When Luis Domingo, the armory sergeant, saw her abilities, he took her under his wing and gave her all the tips he knew for weapon care and firing capability.

After her practice at the range just outside the little town, Flo cleaned her weapon and, as was her nature, began musing about the past.

*Why did I let that b*****d touch me, much less penetrate the sanctity of my body and my soul? I fell for that honeyed tongue of his. I'm glad the butthole is dead! Whoever did it did us all a big favor! And if it was God that did it, I do thank You!*

So many years lost. Lost and no way to ever get them back. She had been robbed of precious years watching her child grow up. HER child. The one she carried and suffered through hours of labor to bring into this world. And she was alone during the whole thing except for a nurse who treated her as if she was a stray cat brought in from the cold. The doctor wasn't much better. She heard him say, "These girls should be fixed so they can never give birth again." THESE girls he called her. Flo didn't know exactly what the doctor meant, but it made her feel degraded and cheap. More so than when that slimy sanctimonious preacher put his sweaty hands on her.

Flo spent years of unending emotional pain wondering was her little girl happy and cared for. Did someone brush her hair and put ribbons in it? Did they cuddle her when she was afraid? Was she told she was smart and pretty? Was she loved? Oh how Flo wished she could have taken back the signing of the adoption papers. She was so young. She really thought this was best for her baby, but was it? The hole in her heart for her lost child had never healed. It haunted her every day and she spent many, many nights crying alone. She could never share her secret with anyone. She knew how she would be thought of. That didn't bother her as much as how people would treat her precious daughter.

Millie never knew that Flo was her mother. Flo knew of the Huckleberry's and asked that they be offered the privilege of adoption. They had sons, but no daughters. The identity of Millie's birth mother was kept from them. The whole town knew that Flo had gone to stay with her aunt in Atlanta, but they all thought that the aunt was in ill health and needed Flo's help.

As Flo gripped her pistol, her anger over the loss of her child grew to a blazing rage. She determined at that moment to tell Millie that she was her mother. Yes! At the very next opportunity, she was going to reveal the secret she had carried so long. And hang the consequences! That rotten Bagston was not going to rule her life anymore!

Asparagus

That thumping at the door could only be the one person who always attacked Charley's door with the heel of his hand, making the door bounce back and forth in its frame.

"Come on in, Luther!"

Charley had been sitting quietly at his kitchen table reading the back of a cereal box, reading-and-eating being a habit of his since childhood. He was getting ready to turn to some passages in the Bible he had been contemplating, which he had only put off because he didn't want to splash milk on the Bible's pages.

Luther poured himself some coffee and sat down.

"What's up?"

"Those wild asparagus ought to be about ready for the picking. And it's a fine day for a walk. Wanna go?"

"Luther, you know I go to church on Sunday. How about you going with me and then we can head out there this afternoon?"

"Nope. Can't do it."

Charley had invited Luther to go to church with him before and always with the same result. Luther would say, "As that great sage Groucho Marx once said…" And Charley would interrupt, "I know, I know." And they would finish as a chorus, "I wouldn't belong to any group that would have me for a member."

"Luther, I'm not asking you to join the church. Just go with me this morning."

"Nope. I know how you Baptists are. Next thing I know, you'd be visiting me at home and praying for me and sending me things in the mail. I'd be meeting people on the street who'd be saying, Brother Luther, we haven't seen you in church lately. You Baptists are like Super Glue. Once I open that tube I'm stuck."

Charley laughed. "It's not that bad and you know it."

They sat quietly and looked around the kitchen.

"Seriously. Why don't you ever go to church?"

"I don't think like you do."

"Explain."

"Pour me another cup of coffee."

"Whoa, whoa! That's plenty. Thanks." Luther took a slurp. "You live in a world that's all divided up and every part is at odds with every other part and there is this big contest going on between the Two Big Parts and it's already set up as to who is going to win and you just have to make sure that you are on the side that is going to make the game-deciding touchdown at the end."

Charley grinned. "Interesting theology, Luther! And what world do you live in?"

"Let's say your divided world is an exclusive world. Meaning only certain people are allowed membership. Others are excluded. That's pretty accurate, isn't it?"

"Well, you are either saved or you are not."

"That's what I mean. It's an exclusive club, your world. There are those who are in and those who are out. The world I live in, Charley, is inclusive. Everybody is in all the time and always has been and always will be."

"Yes, we live in two different worlds. But which one is right?"

"I know what you believe, Charley. You believe the world you believe in is right. I believe they are both right. We live in the two worlds simultaneously. The world of separation and the world of unity. I choose to focus on the world of unity, of the interwhirling, of the great and continuous outpouring of our Source."

"Which reminds me, I'm heading out to pick that outpouring we call asparagus. See you later, buddy!"

Charley sat for a while thinking about what Luther had said. He rose and went looking for a tie.

Report to Godquarters

The Angel of Fire was an emissary of God and as such had direct access to God with instant communication. Their consciousnesses were interwoven. God already knew his report but asked him to enter it into the Archives so others could have access.

> Report of Angel of Fire to Godquarters
> Subject: Current State of Human Consciousness
> Your Majesty and Everlasting Friend,
>
> As per your request, I have entered Earth's atmosphere and assumed the guise of an older male in this small community in what is currently known as the southeastern United States. I am developing a fondness for grits. Lord help me!
>
> A note for the Archives about the state of human consciousness in the year 1428, 2008, 4706, or 5769 depending on whose calendar on earth one is using. There are currently 6,785,608,000 people on earth (and counting). Their birth rate far exceeds their death rate.

Prolific creatures! Akin to rabbits and lemmings in this regard.

Be that as it may, this is a report on the state of human consciousness.

Here are my observations:

1. Each human has a belief system.

2. Each belief in the system is saturated with emotion.

3. Each human's belief system came into being from its experiences with the belief systems of its birth family, its birth community, its birth nation, its birth era.

4. Each human believes its belief system is absolutely the correct belief system.

5. There are 6,785,608,000 belief systems on earth.

6. Each human believes its belief system is correct and the other 6,785,607,999 belief systems range from not quite right to completely wrong.

7. Each human believes its belief system accurately reflects Reality.

8. Each human believes other human's belief systems do not accurately reflect Reality.

9. No one gives attention to this except for a brief moment.

My conclusion is that the current state of human consciousness is still quite primitive. The only thing that saves them from this state of continuous self-absorption is Your Almighty Creative Energy which they call Love.

I should be able to wrap this up this earth year and resume my seat on the Planetary Council.

All Blessings!

Getting Around to Seeing Viola

Millie's opening up to the world around her had been hard work. She didn't trust people in general. Some people didn't deserve her trust. But Flo, Charley, Jeanine, and even Viola were people she had come to confide in. Millie didn't hold to Viola's strange beliefs that seemed too much like witchcraft to her. But Viola was smart in so many ways and Millie didn't want to discount her even though she scared her a little bit.

The gossip around town had grown to have a life of its own. So many folks held it as gospel truth. Some of this gossip had slandered Millie's character. Most of it was about each person's theory on who did in Bro. Bagston, if he was indeed done in. Oh, he deserved it alright. So much of his secret life was not a secret anymore. Didn't seem to bother Mrs. Bagston none. She just held her head high and walked around demanding the respect she had always gotten. She was really good at the game we played as children…Play Like. You know, 'play like' you were a movie star, or 'play like' you were a big green monster just surfaced from the bottom of the lake.

Millie had discussed her theory of murder with Charley some. Seems Charley was getting to be a frequent caller of Millie's. Luther wasn't too happy about this. He had tried to tell Millie that Charley wasn't really interested in her, but Millie thought he sure seemed to be. Guess Luther was just being a big brother and looking out for her.

Millie was putting out some periodicals on the library shelf when Miss Flo came in looking for the latest edition of Paula Deen's magazine. Flo had a mind to try some new recipes and this was a good place to start. Couldn't get any better than good old southern cooking.

"Miss Flo, I've been thinking for some time that I ought to go see Viola."

"Is she sick?" asked Flo.

"No. I mean I want to go talk to her and see if she has the same suspicions as I do about Bro. Bagston's death. She has so much experience with the law, and she seems prone to premonitions."

Flo smiled. "What Viola has are not exactly premonitions. But you are right about her law experience. I'm not sure you should worry yourself so about this murder idea of yours. Maybe you should just let it lie."

Flo found her magazine, muttered about being late for something, and hurried on her way.

Millie thought she was acting mighty peculiar. Maybe she just had a hard day at the store, or maybe she really was in a hurry to try out a recipe. Anyway, Millie wasn't going to be stopped from finding out what Viola thought. And just maybe, Viola could help solve this crime, if it was one.

It didn't take much convincing to get Charley to go along with Millie to Viola's house. He wasn't sure he held to the town gossip about murder, but spending the afternoon with Millie sure appealed to him.

Millie had wanted Flo to go too, but Flo didn't seem too interested. *There just isn't a good reason why Miss Flo wouldn't come with us,* mused Millie. *I finally got the nerve to go and I sure would like her with me.* Viola had known Flo most of her life, so it seemed as though Flo would have no problem talking to her. Oh well, Charley would have to do.

The two of them had no idea what they would walk into when they approached Viola's front door. It was only a day or so ago that Viola had entertained darkness. She was in no mood to talk of frivolous gossip.

Viola invited them in as graciously as she could. She even asked if they needed some sort of refreshment, but they both declined. Millie was too anxious to get to what had been bothering her so long.

"I'm afraid you are going to think I am crazy, Miss Viola. But I really do think that Bro. Bagston was murdered instead of just falling and hitting his head. Since you are so familiar with the workings of law enforcement, I thought you might have some ideas on this."

"Millie dear, I think where humans are concerned most anything is possible. Where Bagston is concerned, I'm surprised that someone hasn't gotten to him long before now."

Viola didn't want to share with Millie everything she knew, but she did want her to know that she agreed with her. "He's been leading a double life for sometime now. In fact, I don't think he ever was what you call a Christian. More like a wolf in sheep's clothing. It pains me to think how many people he has hurt. Why, even Flo….." Viola stopped herself before she spoke too much.

"What about Miss Flo?" Millie asked.

"I just mean that everyone was hurt by Bagston in some way or other."

Millie bought that excuse without another question about it.

"Well, how do we go about proving that Bro. Bagston was killed?"

Millie could not bring herself to address their former preacher in any other way. "Do we question people? Do we start taking statements? Should we call in some of the Atlanta police?"

"Slow down, Millie." Viola saw that Millie was very much in earnest about finding a murderer. She also knew that there were forces at work in this matter that she realized Millie was not able to handle. She wasn't even sure she could handle them.

Viola knew that the visitors she had earlier were certain to come back. She knew they were hard at work devising their evil schemes. In her mind it was her duty to protect those she could from this malignity. It would have to be more power than she had under her control. This kind of power had to come from God Himself.

To calm Millie and help her with the pursuit of a murderer, Viola pledged to aid in any way that she could. She had some friends in the police force in Atlanta and she would call them to come and investigate. They had to be discreet. Any more visitors from out of town would cause a riot of gossip and perhaps impede the investigation. It was not uncommon for friends of Viola's to visit from time to time, and she hoped their presence would be seen as such.

Millie made Viola promise the moment she heard anything. This satisfied her for the moment and excited her at the same time. The walk home with Charley was filled with 'what ifs' and 'who done its'.

Flo Confesses All

The walk to Miss Flo's house was one that became common to Millie. Their friendship had grown beyond bounds. They shared everything, or so Millie thought. As Flo invited Millie in, Millie could see that Flo was not herself. She seemed nervous and distant.

Have I done something to upset her? Is this the end of our friendship? Millie thought to herself as she sat down in one of Flo's comfortable chairs. *No. That's my old way of thinking. I won't let that darkness into my mind.*

She repeated the Bible verse that had come to mean so much to her. *For God hath not given us the spirit of fear; but of power, and of love, and of a sound mind.* She took a deep breath and settled in to listen to her dear friend who seemed to be carrying a heavy burden.

"Millie, I have something to tell you. Something that I should have told you before now. But I never had the courage to." Flo just blurted out her words before she lost her nerve. Millie could sure identify with being afraid to reveal yourself to others.

Flo continued, "Many years ago I had an experience with Bro. Bagston similar to yours."

"Oh, Miss Flo, I'm so sorry. And you've worried about it all these years?"

"Let me finish, Millie. If I don't tell you now, I never will. This may be hard for you to hear, but it's a story that has to be heard to the end. My experience with Bagston went much further than yours. I was caught up with his charismatic manner and his standing in the community. I am ashamed to say that I had a physical relationship with him."

Millie knew her mouth must be hanging wide open. She could find no way to hide the shock in her eyes. However, she understand how persuasive Bagston could be. She was sure all those years ago he must have been a man of good looks.

"I heard my Mama say you left town some years ago to take care of your ailing aunt." Millie was trying to piece together what Flo was telling her and make some sense of it. "Is that why you left?"

"That's part of it. You see, Millie, I was carrying Bagston's child when I left town. My aunt was not sick. That was just something to tell everyone to keep down talk."

Millie could hardly contain her natural curiosity that was running wild. She knew it wasn't polite to ask such personal questions, but she couldn't help herself.

"What happened to the child? Did you leave it in Atlanta?"

"She, Millie, not it. My baby was a little girl. Prettier than anything I had ever seen. The first time I laid eyes on her, I could no longer think of her as a product of sin. She was my baby and I loved her very much. I still love her."

Millie had tears running down her cheeks. That was one of the most touching things she had ever heard. She was touched that someone had shared such an intimate thing with her and bothered by the pain it must have caused Flo to give up her child.

"Did you ever tell her? Does she know you are her Mama?"

"No, Millie. She has never known. I put her up for adoption. She went to a family right here in town. Please understand that I did not want to give her up. At that time, the world was very cruel to an unwed mother and even crueler to the child. I had no one to help me raise her. My parents had passed away sometime before the baby was born."

Millie jumped up from her chair, grabbed Flo by the shoulders, and almost shook her glasses off. "Well, you've got to tell her! She would be so proud to have a Mama like you. She needs to know that you love her and still want her in your life."

Flo cupped Millie's beautiful face in her hands and spoke in a soft tone. "Would you be proud to have me as your Mama?"

"Why yes, but….." Millie stopped in mid sentence as she really looked deep into Flo's eyes. She was almost afraid of what Flo would say next.

"Millie, you are that child I gave up so many years ago. I am your Mama."

The silence seemed to last an eternity as Millie tried to take in what had just been told to her. How could that be? Her Mama was Shirley Huckleberry. Always had been. She was a Huckleberry, with a Mama, Daddy, brothers, and sisters-in-law. Not to mention cousins, nieces, and nephews. Why, there were so many of them they were thought to be a clan. How could she be anybody else?

"Millie, please say something. Do you hate me? Please….say something!"

Millie could not get a hold of her feelings. She just hugged Flo as tight as she could and kept repeating, "You love me. You love me."

Velvet Steel

Ted Wilson was a tough old bird but full of lovingkindness and compassion. He felt genuine affection for every member of the little church and knew them all. He didn't always like the things they did, but he never cut them out of his heart.

Ted loved "every member of the Navel Tribe" as he sometimes put it.

He also had an unrelenting nature, a man of fierce intent. He could be a steel fist in a velvet glove. He tried his best not to hurt anybody (the velvet) but was a force to be reckoned with, not readily overcome (the steel fist).

Ted had a hobby in addition to hiking and long walks and reading the Bible and other books held sacred backward and forward, inside and out. Most folks knew the hiking reading Ted, but not his other hobby.

Not that he kept it secret. Charley, Luther, and Flo knew his other passion well. It was just that most folks saw the exterior and never bothered to know the rest. He didn't mind. He didn't care to know too many folk anyway. He was somewhat of a loner. Much like the main characters of the noir crime novels he loved to read.

Not only were they a welcome contrast to the heavy theological and metaphysical tomes he dived into with such abandon, the hardbitten novels also epitomized a part of him that he didn't often show nor had any reason to. The heroes and heroines were affirmed loners who would assist others but turn away from them just as easily. No attachment. No obligation in either direction.

Ted saw in the novels his own fluid resilience and capability of springing back from any situation. Though he could lament with the best of them, he knew when enough was enough and would quickly be on his way. He felt and intuited deeply, could read a person's soul and character almost instantly, but was rarely swayed by other's emotional energies.

Ted sat firmly in the seat at the center of his soul, not easily moved. Yet he was open to the situation of the moment, and ready to face and deal with whatever arose.

With the trials to come, these qualities would prove their worth for him and his friends on more than one occasion.

Gregor Invades Millie's Dreams

The revealing of Millie as Flo's daughter came to an unfinished end. Millie could not let herself talk more about it. She was in shock. She didn't even remember how she got home. Home…that was a strange word to her now. What exactly was her home? Who were these people who thought enough to adopt her and take her for their own? Who was she to call 'Mama' now? All these questions and more were coming at her like a speeding freight train and she couldn't get out of the way.

She decided that the best thing for her to do was just go to bed and pray that sleep would come. She just couldn't handle any more tonight.

Somewhere around 2:00 am, Millie heard a gravelly voice say, "Don't you know who you are?" She answered, "Yes, I'm Millie. Who I've always been."

She looked around to see who was talking to her. A devilish looking figure stood at the foot of her bed. It was a man. One who wore a hat and spoke with an evil tone. "No. You are an outcast. An unwanted human being. Don't you know who your father is?"

"My father is Herschel Huckleberry."

"No, Millie. Your father is Bro. Bagston! An evil man who only pretended to be a man of God. That's your heritage and that's what you are destined to be."

Millie had been so riveted on Flo being her mother that she had given no thought to who her father was. That sent chills down her spine and made her head hot with fear. This evil creature couldn't be right about her. Bagston could not influence her life anymore than he already had. The thought of him putting his hands on her was sickening. She felt almost grateful to the person who had killed him.

"Ah, got you thinking, huh?" The demonic creature could read her mind. Or maybe he was so used to tormenting humans that he could tell by the expression on her face that he had gotten to Millie.

"I can help you with this, you know," Gregor chuckled. "You just stick with me and we'll make this whole mess come out good for you. I can have people looking up to you. You will be a person of great importance. Just like you have always wanted."

"Go away!" Millie pleaded. "I want no part of you! I know who you are."

"I'll go away now, but you'll want me back soon enough. I'll be around when you need me. I'm always closer than you think." His evil laugh as he vanished was chilling.

"No! I won't need you." Millie shouted. The sound of her own voice woke her. It woke her Papa too. "Millie, are you alright?", he asked as he rushed into her room.

"I'm okay, Papa. It was just a very bad dream."

The Morning After

Millie awoke with the taunts of the evil Gregor coming at her with such evil force that she felt she was being attacked by real beings. If this wasn't a panic attack, she didn't want to know what one was like. Going about her usual morning activities was not possible for her. Shirley Huckleberry called her down to breakfast, but Millie knew she could not swallow one bite. And how could she look the woman she had called Mama for twenty three years in the face?

"Millie, you look pale this morning. Are you alright?" Her Mama was concerned.

"Yes, Mama. I'm alright. I'm just not hungry this morning. I think I'll leave a little early for the library." A little early? It was some three hours before Millie was to report for work.

Millie quickly went out the door, before her Mama could ask any more questions. Shirley called out to Papa. "Herschel, do you know what's wrong with that child of yours?"

"What's Luther done now?" Papa asked as he descended the stairs still wiping the excess shaving cream off his face.

"Not Luther. Millie! She didn't look good and she was acting awfully strange. I couldn't even get her to eat any breakfast."

"All I know is she had a bad dream last night. Maybe it spooked her. She's probably going over to talk to Flo. Maybe that'll give her some peace."

"Flo, Flo, Flo. Always Flo. You'd think she would be able to talk to her own Mama."

Gregor snickered in his evil way as he stood outside the kitchen window and listened in. "Good. My plan is working. These people are so easy."

A Double Remove From Life

Luther and Viola were enjoying an Embassy Suites suite in Atlanta.

"Because we can't!" said Viola. "Or at least I can't, which amounts to the same thing."

"Well, Vi, it's a lot easier for both of us if we just start openly seeing each other and I drop by your house rather than driving all the way up here to Atlanta."

"Easier for you. They'd crucify me."

"Who cares what those people say anyway?"

"I do. I have to make my living in that town." She threw a pillow at him. "I know you don't care. You are already too far gone."

He laughed. "Yep. I don't plan my life around that group. Or any group."

"Well, I do. I have to."

"No, you don't. You only have to if you want to play the society game."

"And what is that according to the gospel of Luther?" she teased.

"You know what it is, Vi. You live your life according to what you think other people think. Kind of a double remove from life itself."

She knew he was right. She also knew from her experience as a counselor that what she thought that other people thought didn't usually match up. Folk mostly just thought about themselves and their situations and rarely thought about other people at all except in the way others affected them. Egocentric was the word. Me, me, me!

People did love a juicy bit of gossip though.

"Where did you go, Vi? What are you thinking?"

"Oh, you are right, Luther! But people in a small town can be pretty judgmental!"

"But what did their Jesus say? Wasn't it let those without sin throw the first stone?"

"Many of them wouldn't stop to think about that, Luther. They would just hurl away. People feel elevated when they put someone else down. And who is going to miss that opportunity?"

"Well, Vi, you can't keep putting yourself down just so other people can feel elevated either. Wanna go get some breakfast?"

Super Size That Please!

Thelma had been wishing for full menopause for some time. She was tired of the curse, as she called it and her mother and grandmother before her. All Eve's fault!

She would have a few dry months of nothing happening and then here it came! In full flow. Like now. She hated it.

Junior didn't need much fine-tuning of his radar to know to stay out of the way. He was heading out the door, as quietly as possible and as far away from Thelma's irritated irrigated state as he could get for a while.

"Junior! Where are you off to now?"

Uh-oh. "Just down to the hardware store to pick up something for that leaky faucet." He was proud of his quick thinking. She wouldn't want to go to the hardware store with him.

"Well, pick me up summa them R. C.'s while you are out. And some Ho Ho's. You know how I lak my Ho Ho's."

"Yes, dear. Okay. Bye."

"An' Junior."

Oh man! He knew he should have left more quickly! "What?"

"Git me a box of Tampons. Super Absorbency."

Junior put his own curse on Thelma with a few choice mumbled words.

"Whut was thet, Junior?"

"I said okay, Thelma."

"And hurry right back, Junior. I need them right away! Super Absorbency, you hear?"

Junior sighed. "Yes, dear."

The screen door slammed.

Junior would feel even worse when he found out what else Thelma was irritated about. Thelma had received some alarming news about Reverend Bagston's death. She didn't know what to do with the information.

Who's My Father?

Millie could not get to Flo's house fast enough. Her mind was racing with thoughts of her birth parents and how would this change her. If people spoke to her on the way, she didn't hear them. She didn't even remember passing Ol' Miss Turner's house. Millie was always afraid to go by there. She usually walked on the other side of the street. Miss Turner had a particularly vicious dog that barked at everyone who passed by. He was a large dog and you never knew if agitated enough that he might be able to jump the small fence around the yard. Today Millie walked by Miss Turner's without even noticing.

Flo was just finishing getting dressed to go to work when she heard a frantic knocking at her front door. She was surprised to see Millie standing there all out of breath and visibly shaking.

"Millie, what in the world is the matter? You look like you just saw a ghost."

"You're not far from wrong, Miss Flo. I had a real scary dream last night. Or at least I think it was a dream."

"Well, sit down over here and get your breath. Let me get you a cup of coffee. That might help."

"No. No, I just had to come over here and get my mind straight by talking to you. This ghost, demon, or whatever he was came to me last night and got me to thinking about some pretty awful things."

"Like what, Millie?" Flo was so glad that Millie had sought her out. She had been afraid that after their last meeting Millie would have nothing to do with her ever again.

"Well, he brought to mind that I was... Oh, I don't even want to say the words! That I was the daughter of Bagston. It makes me purely sick to think about it. But it's true. Everything you told me was true wasn't it?"

"Yes, Millie. It's true. But Bagston is dead now and he can't hurt either one of us anymore. You must consider Herschel Huckleberry as your father now. Rightfully, he's been your only father all along. A father is more than a sperm donor, honey."

"That creature that visited me told me that I was just like him. That was my destiny and I had no way out of it."

Flo walked over to Millie and put her arms around her as any mother would do when a child needed reassurance. "Millie, you are nothing like Bagston and never will be. He was an evil, deceitful man. He hurt many people. You could never be like that. You've had so much come at you at once. It must be so hard for you to handle."

Millie felt herself calming down a little. At least she could breath now without her chest feeling like it was going to explode. "Miss Flo… Mama….oh, I don't know what to call you."

"Whatever you feel comfortable with. It doesn't matter what you call me. Just so we keep our relationship."

"We will," Millie replied. "I feel bad that I came over here with this problem. I should be talking to you or asking you questions about what you've had to go through all these years."

"What's a mother for?" Both of the women laughed with relief. They hugged and Millie felt a sense of belonging that she had never felt before.

Church Conference

It was the custom of the Baptist church to hold a quarterly conference. Fred Perguson, head of the deacon board, had decided that the affairs of the church needed a good looking into. The church treasurer and he had been going over the books. They were more than a puzzlement. There had been some shady goings-on and Bagston had been at the head of it.

The conference was held on a Wednesday night right after prayer meeting. The church was packed. Most of the members were there and some who weren't members. The town gossips had done their job well. Most of the town was here wanting to find out just how much Bagston had hoodwinked them.

"Brothers and sisters," Fred cleared his throat and hesitated before going on. He knew the storm that was coming as he revealed the truth. "First, we need to remember where we are. This is God's house and I don't want there to be any outbursts."

"Oh, come on, Fred. Stop being so all-fired religious on us!" Bill Blackburn was one of the charter members of the church. He was already worked up because he had not been included in the few who knew what was going on.

"Just get on with it."

At that point, Ted Wilson came up front, placed his hand on Fred's shoulder and said, "Folks, Fred has a mighty hard job to do here tonight. Let's don't make it any harder on him. Bill, you just sit there and be quiet. You never have been a man of much patience."

There was a chuckle over the congregation. Fred once again began to speak. "Our Bro. Bagston took most of our building funds and even the missionary fund." Gasps could be heard. Ted once again called for silence.

"Seems our late pastor had a liking for the high life and he used our church money to get it. There are some other sins of his that I don't want to bring up with our good ladies here. Let's just say he fancied himself quite a ladies' man."

Mrs. Bagston couldn't hold it in any longer. "Go on and tell them! He was a womanizer! There were scores of women he knew in the biblical way when he made those trips to Atlanta. You thought he was going on mission business. Well, it was anything but that. He'd come home from one of those trips smelling like booze and cheap perfume. I guess I may as well go on and tell you. He was supporting a pretty hefty drug habit thanks to the funds raised by this church. That's where your bake sale and car wash money went to."

There was certainly silence in the church now. Not even Bill could think of a thing to say. Some of the ladies in the church league had to be escorted out. Bessie Culpepper had actually fainted!

Mrs. Bagston looked around at the folks who had always held her in such high esteem and realized what she had done. She spilled her guts, because her anger at her late husband could no longer be held in.

"Thank you for sharing, Janice." That was all Fred could think to say. How he wished he could faint like Bessie and get out of all this.

"Well, there's one more thing that needs to be said. On those trips to Atlanta that Janice just told us about, Bro. Bagston was making some shady deals with some pretty unsavory characters."

"What kind of deals?" Before Bill could finish his questions the back door of the church flew open. All eyes turned toward the person that came in.

Charley Clears the Room

Charley groaned as he walked through the door. He didn't particularly care for the human species, even though he was a member of the tribe. And he certainly didn't like business meetings. He always had that uneasy sense that it was still the case, just like with Jesus' little band of radical overturners of the status quo, that Judas held the purse strings. Not that Judas was that bad of a guy, really. But he couldn't say that or explore aloud what he meant by that in the general congregation without minds and hearts slamming shut and his standing tried, convicted, and condemned for heresy by many and regarded with confusion and dismay by others. Charley had a section of his mind that was rapidly getting full entitled 'Sermons I Can Never Preach In This Little Baptist Church.' Sometimes he thought, *Why not? Jesus was always upsetting people with what he had to say. Yep. And look what happened to him.* Charley felt he was not as brave as Jesus.

Charley's heart sighed and groaned as he made his way to a front pew seat. Though he didn't much care for the human species, he loved each person, each individual. He could see the spark of the Divine in each one. He always talked to that spark, rather than the swirl of emotions, the platitudes, the justifications, the poses and stances, the angers and denials that looked to obscure the spark, even put it out.

As he moved through the congregation down the central aisle, Charley had to breathe out strong clear spiritual energy to get through the thick clouds of feeling that folk had brought with them to the meeting, that were filling and polluting the atmosphere of the room. Charley went out of his mind, out of his emotions, out of all self-reflection and settled more deeply into the calm of the Light at his core.

Fred Perguson looked at Charley with great relief and said, "Charley, come on up here. We need you to help us get started." Fred promptly sat down.

Charley stood quietly. He looked up and said, "The first thing we have to do is clear the room."

Some folk looked confused (*"but we just got here"*). Others, there as curious visitors, were shifting into obstinacy and anger (*"who does he think he is? he can't make me leave"*). Ted laughed with pleasure at Charley's opening statement. He knew exactly what Charley meant.

"Will everyone please stand up?"

"Come on. Come on. Trust me, it's not going to hurt you."

People began standing. Charley stood quietly until everyone stood. He knew the power of social pressure and used it when necessary.

Charley also knew that when people shifted their physical position, they shifted their perspective. They saw things around them just a little differently. They sometimes even saw things they hadn't seen before. The atmosphere in the room was beginning to change already.

Another important part of his simple request was that in obeying it, people had done two things. They had submitted themselves to Charley's will, at least temporarily, allowing him to guide the meeting. And they had shifted from being a mob to an orderly group.

"Even though we have some very important business to discuss, maybe even especially because, that doesn't mean we let who we are and the way we usually do things just slide away. So let's just take a few moments. We have folk here we haven't seen in a while and some new folks too. Take some time right now to greet your neighbors. Let's see some of that Baptist hospitality!"

The room became a buzz of hellos and how are yous and hand shakings and smiles of welcome.

As folk were just about through, Charley did not allow them time to think, time to regress to the way they had been a few minutes ago. He said, "Flo, will you lead us in a word of prayer?"

Flo sat frozen to her seat. She, along with everyone else, could not believe that Charley had called on her to pray. Maybe she just thought she heard her name called. After all, women weren't usually asked to pray in the sanctuary. And Flo had not darkened the door of this church since she left it more than twenty-three years ago. She wasn't even a member anymore. What was Charley thinking?

Flo....?" Charley said her name once more. Louder this time. There was no mistaking.

Rising to her feet, Flo began her prayer. "Lord, we ask you to help us remain calm here today. And rid us of the spirits of anger, revenge, and judgment. Help us to see that this meeting is about the loss of money that was freely given to You. Not about our personal money. We ask you to give us wisdom to know what to do now. How do we handle this problem, Lord? We need your guidance. Amen."

No one had seen Gregor and two of his evil cronies as they had made their way around the church whispering in the ears of those assembled there. They had stirred up a pack of trouble. They laughed to themselves about how easy it was to get these humans stirred up. Why, look what they had gotten Mrs. Bagston to confess. A few well chosen words whispered in her ear and she totally forgot about her precious standing in the community.

As Flo finished her prayer, two spiritual beings standing on the sidelines moved into quick action. The Angel of Light and the Angel of Fire had been given the command to remove Gregor and his fiends.

"Let's go, guys. It's them!" Gregor growled as they headed outside. "They think they are so superior," one of the demons snarled. "Well, they are," Gregor answered. "But we're not done yet. We have a lot more work to do. But not now."

An Idea Is Born

Charley once again began to speak to the crowd. "We have already heard how Bagston robbed the church of most of its money. The church bonds are only worthless paper now. But we can in time replace what we have lost. We have a bigger problem to discuss. As we heard, Bro. Bagston spent a good deal of time in Atlanta. We have found out that while there he made some shady deals with the mob."

Loud gasps rose up with Charley's news. How much more could this group of small town people stand to hear?

"Now settle down, folks. We have a serious problem hanging over us and we must keep our wits about us. We are in serious danger of losing our church and the property it stands on."

"I've been giving this a lot of thought and prayer and meditation and some ideas have come to me. Seems to me we need to do two things. One, the most important from my view, is to deepen and strengthen the spiritual life of us as individuals and us as a spiritual community."

"Amen!" rang out spontaneously from all directions.

"The other is to raise money to pay off these debts we find ourselves in."

Not so many amens rang out on that one.

"Come on now. Baptists are good at raising money. Why do you think we stand up and sing when we take up the offering? So you can reach down deep into those pockets!"

Laughter rolled through and with it came its sister, Light.

"How do we do this, Charley?"

"Well, Ed, I'm glad you asked. I think we can do both of these things at once."

"Both things? What's the other thing, Charley?" Miss Evelyn had been focused on if and when Charley was going to give an altar call which she felt she sorely needed, wanting to go down and turn it all over to the Lord again.

"Why, deepen our spiritual life and raise money! I think we can do both at once."

"Now you are starting to sound like those Episcopalians!" Arthur Garfield snorted, half-jokingly. Folk rolled their eyes upward and groaned, being more open to interfaith harmony rather than that old style berating and putting others down so one could feel superior.

"Maybe they'd be willing to join in with us!" said Charley, making Arthur's eyes roll upward now.

"Come on, Charley! What's your idea?"

"A preach-off ! A preach-off, with all day singing and dinner on the grounds."

Preach-off!

A preach-off! What exactly was this? Charley could see the puzzled looks and heard the growing buzzing as folks had just taken in what he said.

"Hold on. I'm going to explain what I mean. To have a preach-off we mail out flyers to as many preachers as we want. Those who accept the offer to come here to our little church will also agree to let our church have all the offering taken up at their service. We'll use that money to pay off our debts and save our church. The bigger name preacher we have here, the more money we raise."

"Charley, do you think some of those big name preachers will come here? Why would they want to?"

"They'd come. Some to help a struggling church out of their trouble. Some would come to spread the gospel and win lost souls. And some to make a bigger name for themselves by winning the preach-off."

"And how would they win?"

"The preacher who draws the biggest crowd and makes the most money for us would be the winner."

"Don't you mean we would be the winner, Charley?" Bill couldn't resist getting a laugh out of folks.

"Exactly! Now you've caught on to why we would have this in the first place. Let's put it to a vote. Those in favor of a preach-off raise your right hands." Of course, everyone raised their hands. Who could pass up an opportunity to hear some of this nation's finest preachers?

"Alright. Let's do this the right way. Those opposed raise your right hands."

No one was opposed. They were already seeing the money pouring in. Why, this would be a big boon to the local businessmen, too. You could feel the excitement as they began to chatter to each other. They were slapping each other on the back and acting as if they had won the lottery.

" Now before you folks leave, we'll have a piece of paper up front on the communion table. Those of you who have a preacher in mind, come up front and put their names on the list. The leadership here will get together and invite all those mentioned. Start spreading the word." Charley knew he didn't have to tell them that. They were already whipping out cell phones and rushing out to tell everyone they saw. He knew it was no use to have a closing prayer for their meeting. He'd never get them quiet enough to do that now.

Gregor's Plot

The local townsfolk weren't the only ones rushing out of the conference with big plans in mind. No one could see them, but Viola felt them as they ran by her. Gregor and his fellow demons were charged up now!

"Come on, guys! We've got a lot of work to do." Gregor could hardly control himself. Control wasn't one of his strong suits anyway. "I can't believe these humans. They've set themselves up for destruction this time. By the time we've finished, they will be at each others throats. They'll lose this church and the big guys will have their casino built."

Gregor wasn't about to fail in his mission. He knew what happens to demons who fail. It would be "the Pit" for them. He had already lost out on his plans for Millie and Viola. Those two women proved to be stronger than he thought. Certainly not as effortless as Bagston had been.

The ease with which Gregor viewed the church's demise made him rather cocky. He could just see himself being made chief among demons. "Gregor?" One of his devilish friends trying to get his attention brought him back to reality. "Gregor, what's the plan? What's our first move?"

"Well, first we've got to make sure which preachers are called to this preach-off. We don't want any of those take-the-Bible-literally preachers. They want to teach the Word of God like it's real and true. Yes sir, we can't have any of those around here."

"Then, we've got to get these humans mad with each other. So they don't talk *to* but *about* each other. That shouldn't be hard to do. They'll be squabbling over who's going to be the best preacher. And whose preacher will raise the most money. Then we'll have them fighting over how to spend the money. Oh, there's all kinds of ways to mess with these frail beings. We need to get our plan in order. Unless you boys just like darkness and heat, you'd better do your best work."

Will The Real Millie Please Stand Up?

Most all of her life Millie had longed to be someone else. Anyone other than herself. She wasn't particularly sure of who she was, but she was sure of what she was not supposed to be. She was often told not to show anger, not to be outspoken, not to express her opinion on anything and especially not to let anyone know her thoughts. In her mind, doing this would reveal that she was some defective alien creature. Someone so different from others in the world that, if they had really known her, she would be even more ostracized than she felt herself to be.

What Millie really needed was to be exactly who she is. Not conforming to others expectations, or even to her own. To be what

God had created her to be. A unique individual. She always took this negatively as if she were someone weird.

How could she come to know the real Millie? She needed to learn the real freedom in being who God had made her to be. It reminded her of watching her brother perform his karate moves in their backyard. She would sit on the back steps and watch as he went through his time of practice. He moved with such unencumbered freedom, with such impressive grace and style. It could almost be put to music. But she knew that each movement was either in defense of one's self, or to bring harm to a predator.

That's it! To move through life with grace (God's grace) and purpose (God's purpose). Never mind what anyone else thought. She became aware that she even had to shed the image that she had imposed on herself. Maybe, just maybe, the concept she thought others had of her was partly her fault. It hit her that she had been living in a prison of her own making. She had chosen to give value to the opinions of other frail humans. She had been the main player in keeping those opinions alive.

Well, heck fire! She was just going to be who she is in each moment. Without dragging all those negative thoughts of herself into every current situation. Just the idea of that made her carry herself in an entirely different way. She felt taller and a lot lighter having chosen to lay down all that old garbage. But just like her brother's karate, it would take much practice.

As the Bible says, "If God be for us, who can be against us?" (Romans 8:31). God loved Millie just as she is. If the Creator of the universe could love her and count her valuable, then what did it matter what imperfect mankind thought?

Charley Calls a Meeting

Charley knew someone had to have a sense of order about the preach-off. He could see that everyone was so excited, but had their own ideas of who could speak. As acting pastor, it was his responsibility to see that things didn't get out of hand.

He gave it some thought and came up with who would be likely candidates for a Credentials Committee. Himself, of course, Brother

Ted, Flo, and Mrs. Bagston. Knowing there had to be an uneven number on the committee, Charley tried to come up with someone who would present a different viewpoint. Miss Evelyn!! Now there's different for you! He contacted each prospective member and set up a meeting for the very next night.

Ted was pleased to receive the invite from Charley. That young man was a step ahead most of the time! Ted gave Flo a call to see how she was reacting to being on the committee and to get some understanding of her thoughts. *Always good to know people's minds ahead of time*, he thought.

Flo was busy cleaning house when the phone rang. She did love to keep her house neat. "Hello. Is that you, Ted?"

Ted was kind of startled, "Yes, how did you know?"

Holding back the laughter, Flo answered, "I've got caller id. Hang on a minute, Ted. I also have call waiting." And she was gone.

Ted thought, *This world, this world! These young folk will dump you in a moment if someone new comes along.*

"Ted?"

"I'm here, Flo."

"Sorry about that."

Heaving an impatient sigh Ted replied, "Do you have a few moments (hoping she wouldn't go leaping to some new attraction for a while). I wanted to see what you thought about the credentials committee. I understand you are on it, too."

"I think it's a great idea, Ted. We need to have some kind of framework for such a large event."

Agreeing with her, Ted asked Flo to share some of her thoughts.

"Well, I know we are a relatively conservative church, but I'd like to open it up to more than just the usual pastors that do the revivals around here."

Flo had gotten Ted's attention. "Do you have some others in mind?"

"Take a deep breath, Ted. (Both laughed) I'd like to allow some women to have a chance."

When Janice Bagston got the call from Charley, she readily agreed to be on the committee. Though she was mighty disappointed that she could not be the chairwoman, or maybe that should be the chairman. She was beginning to feel her independence since her controlling husband was gone. Even if she could not be the head in name, she was sure she could have things her way.

Miss Evelyn got the call from Charley just about the time she was going to put supper on for her husband, Jim. Now supper was just going to have to wait. Instead of burning supper, as she was prone to do, Evelyn was burning up the phone lines calling every woman she knew in the congregation and those in town too. "I have been CHOSEN!" she said with pride.

"They chose ME! I guess they thought they could not do without me." Little did she know that she was just an afterthought of Charley's. But this was her crowning hour and she was not going to let it slip past the notice of anyone.

The night for the meeting came and Charley had chosen to meet in the ladies Sunday School room. He thought that might put some of the ladies at ease. He had no idea what he was in for from these women.

Evelyn arrived before the others. She was excited and fully prepared. She had baked some cookies which were universally detested because of the large amount of baking soda she used. She also had a large supply of grape Kool-Aid in two Tupperware pitchers and five clean jelly glasses with a 'Credentials Committee' label taped on each.

As Charley entered the room, followed by the other committee members, he spied the refreshments Evelyn had brought. She was just about to serve up some for everyone. "Evening, Evelyn. I see you have brought some of your cookies for us. But this is a very serious matter we are to undertake tonight. Perhaps we should save your refreshments for after the meeting."

Flo, Ted, and Janice gave a sigh of relief. It was up to them now what kind of excuse they gave to get out of eating those horrendous cookies. Ted and Flo almost simultaneously made noises about just having had a large supper and didn't know if they could eat another bite.

Janice Bagston wasn't studying eating of any sort. She was here to express her opinions and to see that everyone knew just where she stood. She was anxious to get the meeting started. Flo could see the tension in Janice's face and body. She looked like a woman with a mission. *Hmmm. This could be an interesting evening,* thought Flo. *We might have a lively night.*

Charley began by thanking each one for consenting to being on the committee. "I felt sound minds should prevail in this matter." He knew what he was saying when he said 'sound' minds. Miss Evelyn didn't exactly fit into that category, but his Southern manners took over.

"You are welcome, Charley." Ted agreed that a credentials committee was needed for this event. "We need to get our part settled before any invitations or news releases or anything else can happen. Charley, what do you see as our next order of business?"

"I think we should give serious consideration to just what kind of preachers we ask to our preach-off." Charley then asked for ideas from the group.

Flo started to answer, but Janice talked over her in a commanding voice. "I think we should have someone here with a few different viewpoints than what we have been used to hearing!" Knowing she was talking about her late husband, everyone agreed. "There should be someone more respectable, more honest. I even think we should consider a woman."

Evelyn almost spilled the whole pitcher of Kool-Aid on her prized cookies. She choked so hard that Ted had to pat her on the back until she caught her breath.

Flo was mighty pleased to hear Janice say this. It made Flo's views a little easier since the ice was already broken, and in Evelyn's case on her lap. But Flo decided to play it a little cool. She wanted to see where Janice was going with this.

"Evelyn, are you okay now?" Janice didn't want to go on until she had everyone's attention.

Evelyn could only nod her head. What had she gotten herself into? Why had she made it public that she was on this committee? How was she going to explain this to the women's church league?

Janice continued, "Well, I think women have not been given their rightful place in this church. It was okay for us to do the cooking, cleaning up and such. Even the Vacation Bible School was given to us, though I never cared for spending two full weeks with all those screaming kids. It's time we women were given a voice."

Ted and Charley thought to themselves that most of these women already had a voice and weren't afraid to use it.

"But what about the doctrine that women should be seen and not heard?"

"Oh grow up, Evelyn! Don't you know your Bible? The first person to spread the gospel was Mary when she found Jesus' tomb empty." Janice was feeling very superior right now.

Evelyn thought, *You bitch! In your case it's the womb that is empty.* But she said, "No need to get that way, Janice. After all we are all Christians here."

Charley could see a fight coming. "Now ladies, let's remember why we are here. It's good to see that everyone has an opinion on this matter. And that we aren't afraid to express it. But let's keep on the subject."

"I like the idea myself. How about we put that on the board there? At least for the sake of discussion. It'll keep us on track." Ted volunteered to keep the board. "Now let's see. Qualifications… no gender discrimination. Okay?"

All agreed. At least for now.

Even Evelyn agreed. She didn't want to be the only one against. After all, they might kick her off the committee. That would be more than she could stand. How would she show her face in town after this?

"Anyone have any ideas about the other qualifications for our preachers? Ted, how about you?" Charley was looking for his friend to help him keep the women from killing each other. "Before you begin, let me ask all of you to keep in mind that this is a church. We don't want anyone preaching here that we would not ordinarily invite. We do have to keep our biblical standards."

"Do you think we are going to be held accountable for what anyone says from the pulpit? How's that been working for us? We need to come out of our sanctimonious fog and get people to think for themselves. They can't get to heaven on someone else's coat tails. Time they woke up!"

"Janice, I appreciate your zeal, but I believe it's Bro. Ted's turn to speak." Charley was trying as hard as he could to keep control of this meeting.

Ted took a minute to be sure Janice had not taken another breath to begin again. "Charley, are we going to allow folk from other denominations to preach?"

"I don't see why not. We do have to show some caution though. Don't you think?"

Flo spoke up, "That's something that bothers me. I don't know where the caution line is. I mean I know we don't want murderers and rapists and so on. That's pretty obvious, but I don't know enough theology to make judgment calls on whether folk have pure Baptist doctrine or not."

"Well, I do think we need people to follow our teachings!" Everyone saw Evelyn sit up tall and get that 'I'm better than anyone else' look as she spoke.

Janice couldn't hold it in this time. "OUR teachings? What in the world are you talking about, Evelyn?"

If they don't follow our teachings, we can give them a bag of your cookies. Flo wished she could say it out loud, but she didn't.

"Well, I think Evelyn has put her finger on it even though I wouldn't phrase it that way." Ted gave a knowing look at Charley. "For example, we have a fellow who has been pretty demonic in his life but has been redeemed. He wants to preach. We've got some tough calls to make."

Concerned about the time and ready to end his misery, Charley spoke up. "I can see that this could take all night and all day tomorrow. So, let's just decide on some basic guidelines tonight and go with that. All agreed? Okay. So far we say men or women, no murderers, and no rapists. Any other no's?"

Ted saw this as a good time to bring up those he wanted to add to the list. "I know this is a hot topic, but there are some really decent, good-hearted, Jesus loving people out there who live with and love folk of their own gender."

Evelyn nearly fell off her chair. "Ew! Ugh! How can you even bring that up?"

Charley felt he had to say something since he *was* the pastor. "Now, Ted, I usually go along with what you say, but I think that's going a little too far. Some people in this town would burn this church down if we tried that."

"I know. Violence is much more approved of than sex." Ted was shaking his head as he spoke.

"Well, Ted, that's just the way it is. We are a Bible-based church and we should stick to it. Remember, this whole thing is to raise money for the church. Some people are mighty funny who they give their money to."

"There is one of those boundaries right there...money," Flo pointed out. "Just because some folk won't give their money is no reason to blacklist good folk."

"Speaking of blacks, are we going to allow them to preach?"

"Nice move to change the subject, Eve." You could hear the disgust in Flo's voice. Evelyn kind of gave a half grin and sank down in her chair. Janice wished Evelyn would put one of her big ol' cookies in her mouth and choke on it.

Ted wrote "gays", "blacks", and "old people" on the board with question marks after each.

Janice just glared at Ted, "You wrote that 'old people' up there just to be funny, didn't you Ted?"

"Well, yeah... kinda. And there is ageism around too. What do you think about all this, Janice?"

"I wouldn't know. I'm still very young!"

Ted wrote Janice's name on the board and gave her a point.

Once again, Charley had to step in to avoid a free-for-all. "I can see that this meeting is not going to end on an agreeable note. My suggestion is we meet again after we get applications from speakers. We can then go over them individually and see if we can come to some kind of agreement. Anyone second that motion?"

"Charley, that's kind of a copout, but I can see the wisdom in it. It also gives us time to lobby each other for maybe some mind changing."

Flo was already thinking of who she could convince to vote her way.

Charley knew he wouldn't get away with shifting the subject, but Flo's suggestion for lobbying seemed to appeal to the others. It sure got Janice and Evelyn fired up.

"As I understand it, our job as the credentials committee (and, Evelyn, can we keep these jelly glasses?) is to make these tough decisions. All we have decided so far is both men and women can preach.

"I guess you're right, Ted. But I think this is all we can agree on tonight." Charley was anxious to put this meeting to an end. "Do I hear a motion?"

Ted knew that Charley had a hot date with Millie so he didn't put up any more fuss. "I so move."

"All agreed, say aye."

"Anyone opposed?" None.

Thank you, Lord, Charley said to himself. *How in this world did I get into this mess. I just had to suggest a preach-off!*

Ted and Charley

Ted pulled Charley aside after the others had gone. "Charley, will you be calling another committee meeting?"

"Yeah. But just between you and me, I wish I had taken longer to think about the people I chose. I know I wanted a variety of opinions, but I didn't count on having a major debate at every meeting. And what's up with Evelyn and those cookies? What kind of meeting did she think we were having? Ted, I'm telling you, I'd just as soon chuck this whole idea of a preach-off."

"Oh, Charley, that was just the first meeting. Everybody had to say their piece. They won't be so bad next time. Everybody but Janice, that is. I think she's wound up over something and hasn't said it yet. And then there's Evelyn and her cookies. She means so well, but is divided in herself. I guess she figures she has to give people things all the time just to be accepted."

"Maybe. But by doing that she just makes it harder for people to accept her! Anyway, it is what it is. Too late to go back now. I only hope that we can get through this thing without someone getting hurt."

"Charley, my boy, that's not possible, but I think we can let each other know we might disagree but still have appreciation for each other. I certainly hope that's so."

"You really think Janice Bagston will buy that?"

"I don't know what Janice will buy. I'm kinda concerned about her. She's been put down so long. Like a compressed spring suddenly released, she could fly in most any direction."

Charley chuckled at Ted's description. "Yeah, she's a lit stick of dynamite alright. You won't believe the rumors I have heard about her latest activities."

"O lord, Charley, just go ahead and tell me. Don't make me beg."

"We sound like a couple of old ladies at the women's church league." Both laugh.

"Okay, here goes. It seems Janice has been frequently visiting that male strip club up near Atlanta. One of our "good" members saw her there. Said she was drunk as a skunk and stuffing dollar bills into every Speedo there."

"What's a Speedo?" Ted was showing his age.

"It's one of those tight thong things guys wear. Tight enough to reveal everything." Charley was real uneasy discussing such things, especially with Ted.

"Oh, I see. What we used to call a jock." Now Ted was really showing how old he was.

Charley began to be really uncomfortable. "I suppose. It doesn't come up in my conversations very often."

"Me either, Charley. Let's get back to Janice. Bless her heart you know she must be hurting with all she's gone through. Is there anybody close to her that she trusts?"

"Viola seems to be the only one lately to approach her without walking away with claw marks."

"Viola would be the one who could do that alright. I have a lot of respect for that woman."

Charley agreed. "She's not your typical example of a 'church lady', but I like her too. I think Janice can talk to her without being judged."

"Well Charley, if you are planning to call another meeting soon, I'll try to behave."

Charley cracked up laughing. "That felt good. Quite a relief to laugh like that. As soon as we get in a few applications, I think we should meet. I'm sure they will come pouring in. In fact, some people have already given me a few names. So, I don't think we should let too much time go by until our next meeting. Probably at the end of this week. What do you think?"

"You just let me know, Charley, and I'll be there. I appreciate you chairing this. You are the right person for it."

"Is this where I'm supposed to say thanks? I know what you mean though."

"Charley I'm gonna keep appreciating you until you accept it so you might as well get used to it." Ted was laughing as he spoke.

"Ted, you just keep on being here, and please find some way to keep me from having to eat those awful cookies of Evelyn's."

"Okay, Charley, I'll give some thought to it. Talk with you later."

"Counting on it, Ted. See ya."

Viola Investigates

Viola had taken the visit from Charley and Millie seriously. Probably more seriously than they expected. She had her own doubts as to how Bro. Bagston met his end. She certainly had the resources and know-how to conduct an investigation. Using her skills seemed like something she would really enjoy. It had been some time since she had worked on a criminal case. Besides, it would help her forget Luther's suggestion to let the whole world know about their relationship. That was not something she was willing to do right now. Maybe never.

Her first call would be to her connections at the Atlanta Police Department. During all the years her father had worked there most of the detectives had watched her grow up. They were more than willing to give Viola any advice or assistance she might need. After a lengthy conversation with Captain Jerrard, she began to plan her strategy to get to the bottom of Bagston's murder, if in fact that's what it was. Captain Jerrard had listened as Viola gave him as many details as she could of the pulpit dive. She was careful not to put too much emphasis on any one detail, but to just relay the facts as she knew them. Town gossip could play no part in a good investigation.

Jerrard said the matter indeed warranted investigation. He offered help by anyone on the force that Viola thought she needed. Viola explained that discretion on their part would be mighty important in this small town. Someone getting a new haircut would cause a whirlwind of talk. A murder investigation by the big city police would cause a tornado. They both agreed that everything would be handled low-key.

Viola had two people in mind to interview. Flo and Janice Bagston. She knew Janice had to be handled carefully. Janice's present state of mind was volatile to say the least.

Viola had not paid her 'sympathy call' on Janice, so perhaps this was a way to get in the door and see if Janice was open to talking. These southern ways did have their advantages. Janice would not think it strange at all for Viola to drop by. Janice probably had a checklist, if not on paper for sure in her head, as to who had come by to pay their respects and who had not.

Viola went out to her backyard to cut a few flowers to take over. She had learned quickly that front yard flowers were not to be cut but kept for viewing by all who passed by. And my, did a lot of people pass by! Everyone of them had a remark to make on the state of her grass and flowers and plenty of advice on what she might do better.

Janice had been spending her morning in the usual way. One that was not known to the community. At least, she hoped not. She had been exercising to one of those videos she had seen advertised on TV. She had let herself go so long and was wanting to make up for years of neglect to her body. After all, how was she going to catch a man? She had the music up loud and almost didn't hear the doorbell.

When she finally heard it, she frantically reached for a robe to cover up the fuchsia leotard she was wearing. "I'm coming! I'm coming!"

Viola heard the music crank down. It had been so loud that Janice's windowpanes were rattling. Viola grinned. *Well at least she's letting loose!*

"Hi, Janice. Is this an okay time to stop by?"

Janice had almost not been able to switch from "Sweating to the Oldies" to grieving widow. When she saw Viola at the door, she felt a panic attack coming on. "Why no, Viola. It's always a pleasure to see you. Come on in. Can I offer you some iced tea?"

Viola thought that Janice looked as if she were about to have an attack of the vapors. Viola had heard that southern women were prone to such but always thought it was just a prejudiced rumor. What Viola didn't know was that a good case of the vapors had always been a way of escape for Southern women from an unpleasant conversation or a distasteful chore.

"I'd love some tea. It's turning out to be one of those sweltering days. Was that "Sweating With The Oldies" I just heard? It's one of my favorite exercise videos. You know it's a shame this town doesn't have a gym for women."

"Why, no. I was just listening to some of the oldies from my high school days. It brings back such pleasant memories and helps me in my time of grief. Whatever makes you think the ladies of this town would want to go into a sweaty old gym? I certainly wouldn't. Not in the frame of mind I've been in."

"Well Janice, I kind of lost touch with you. There's been so much going on, we've all been in different frames of mind lately."

"Isn't it a shame that we are all so busy?" Janice wished she could just drop the well-mannered, grieving widow act and be herself with Viola. But could she really trust her?

"What brings you here today, Viola. I see you have a lovely bunch of flowers with you. I hope you did not cut them from your front yard."

Viola saw that she would have to resort to more drastic measures with Janice and was not adverse to doing so. When she reached across Janice's iced tea to get some more sugar, she opened a hidden compartment of her ring and dropped an odorless, tasteless, instantly dissolvable fast-acting truth potion in Janice's tea.

Janice took some long slow sips from her tea. This not only helped her cool down but delayed answering any questions that Viola might have. Janice knew that Viola was a smart cookie and it would be hard to fool her. Little did she know that truth would begin pouring from her like sweat had just been pouring into her fuchsia leotards.

Viola sat back in the overstuffed chair Janice offered her and waited for the potion to take effect.

Janice said, "I've heard those rumors about me. Yes, I've been up to Chippendales in Atlanta. My brother Bobby dances there. How that has stayed a secret so long in this little town I don't know. And, yes, I had a couple of beers one night while waiting for Bobby to get off work. So what?"

Viola wasn't all that interested in Janice's life as a minister's wife in a small southern town. She wanted to know about the events surrounding Bagston's death, but she figured that Janice would eventually get around to that.

(Meanwhile Evelyn was busily baking more cookies; Gregor was polishing up his sermon for the preach-off; Charley was spooning Millie who was appreciating his silverware; Ted was completing his reading of *Sources of the Self: The Making of the Modern Identity*; Jeanine Bulloch was wondering why she had been introduced into the novel then dropped like a hot tamale; Thelma was thinking up things for Junior to do; Junior was conveniently going deaf; Luther was out on an extended hiking camping trip.)

Janice went off on a rant. "Viola, you have no idea what I've been through. Neither does anyone else. Oh, they have their gossip and their smears where they talk about me going wild. Well, the gossipers are the ones that worked so hard to put me in a little preacher wife box in the first place! And like a fool I went along with it! I'm tired of being a little bobble-headed, oh-what-a-saint-she-is doll, nodding my head to everybody else's wants and wishes and demands. I'm not doing it anymore!"

Janice was pacing around the room now, her eyes flaming. "Do you think I actually liked being married to Bagston? I couldn't stand the man! I tried, Lord knows I tried to get his attention. I even went to the old swamp woman to get her famous love potion. And don't you dare laugh, Viola! I have needs too. Needs that I fully intend to see satisfied."

"Bless your heart, Janice! Its so good to hear you saying what you truly think and feel." Viola didn't get easily shocked by what most folks said. But hearing this talk of love potions and satisfaction come out of Janice's mouth left her stunned. She would have to turn the conversation to murder if she could.

Janice now shifted to ripping her late husband to shreds.

"Janice, since we are talking about Preacher Bagston, have you ever given thought to just how he really died. Have you ever had any reason to question?"

"I'm afraid to talk about that." Janice put the tips of her fingers on her mouth as if deep in thought.

"Why would you be afraid? He's dead and gone."

"He was doing different drugs you know. I don't know if he overdosed or if he was killed."

"So you have thought about him being murdered? What makes you think that?"

"Bagston was mixed up with all kind of folk who wouldn't hesitate at murder if they thought they had been double-crossed or wronged."

"Just what kind of folk was he mixed up with? I know you said he did some gambling and a lot of womanizing. But what else?"

"He had some kind of dealings with the owner of the club where my brother Bobby dances. Marlon Mayhew."

Viola recognized that name from conversations with her friends at the Atlanta Police Department. Mayhew was not the kind of man you wanted to be connected with. The police had never been able to pin anything on him, but several people had come up missing after dealings with him."

Janice said, "You know that man Freddy that came to town? I think he came to see you. He works for Mayhew."

Viola thought to herself *I knew that man was up to no good. He was probably trying to find out what I know.* "Janice, who do you think murdered your husband? Some people think you might have had something to do with it."

"Those bitches!!! and that Evelyn Sanctimony is the worst of the lot!"

"Well, I can't disagree with that. I'm surprised that she hasn't killed someone already with those cookies of hers."

Janice laughed. "Viola, you are a breath of fresh air. Maybe she killed Bagston. I can tell you that I didn't have anything to do with his murder. Sometimes I wish I had. My best guess would be that he crossed Mayhew one time too many. I heard him talking on the phone once to some real estate agent. He was bragging about how he had bamboozled some powerful people into thinking he was going to see that they got the church property."

"I hate to ask you this because I don't want to alarm you needlessly, but Janice, do you know anything or have access to anything that might make those folk see you as a threat?"

"I don't know. I suppose there could be some papers in the house that might be incriminating to them. Bagston kept a locked file in his study. He absolutely forbid me to go into his study. I haven't gone in there because it reminds me too much of him. Do you think we ought to see what's there?"

"Indeed I do, Janice. I think that is a good idea." But that would have to wait until another day.

Second Committee Meeting

The Credentials Committee, all spirited folk, were beginning to feel their power. Bagston's demise had created a vacuum and they had decided they were the ones to fill it. Jeanine Bulloch, as Evelyn's replacement, sat uneasily, not knowing what to expect.

Janice was still getting practice in being released from the role of minister's wife. Lately she had been feeling her freedom and stretching her newly found muscles. In the past she had had run-ins with Jeanine and her fundamentalist mind-set. She fired a broadside over Jeanine's bow. "Charley, I see that Evelyn didn't want to be in our group anymore. I'm happy to see Jeanine here because she's a real Christian."

"Now Janice, we don't need any sarcasm. We have some serious things to take care of."

Ted was anxious to get down to business. "How do you see us conducting our business here today, Charley? Do we need to get Jeanine caught up to speed?"

Jeanine smiled at her inclusion. "Charley and I have already met about this. He pretty much got me caught up. Besides I don't think you were able to come to many decisions. Am I right?"

Janice saw an opening and went for it. "Now Jeanine, we don't need any sarcasm. Didn't you hear?"

Charley sighed. "Now ladies, let's be nice."

"It's true we didn't get much settled last time," Ted explained. "It seemed like we were mostly just getting used to the idea that we had quite a bit of responsibility here. What we decide can pretty much determine the tone of the whole preach-off."

Charley took command. "Have any of you been able to give the preach-off much thought since our last meeting? I would love to hear any ideas you might have. Not just about who preaches, but maybe the tone of the whole thing."

Jeanine jumped in. "I know I'm the newest member of this committee, but we've all known each other for a long time, so I won't be shy. I think we need some good solid preachers that will draw a respectable, yet sizable crowd. Preachers that will nourish us in our faith."

"Jeanine, I think that is exactly what we need." Flo sat back in her seat and crossed her arms. "We got a little wild last time and entertained the idea of having a woman preacher and maybe some not so conventional ones. But we don't want to seem like we are trying to run a sideshow here."

Charley said, "Flo, I'm surprised you might think having a woman preacher would be like running a sideshow."

"That's not exactly what I said. At least that's not what I meant. I just think we shouldn't be trying to have a religious cook-off here. I don't think this is supposed to be about forcing doctrine on anyone. We are doing this to save our church."

Ted laughed. "A religious cook-off! I like that, Flo." All laughed except Janice kind of snurkled. Ted continued, "That part about not forcing doctrine on anyone, though, cuts both ways. We might think about the diversity of congregation we hope to attract, if we want more than just our usual attendees."

Jeanine rolled her eyes and sighed. "I guess all of us have a point to make. We do want to draw a good crowd. I just think we need to remember that this is a church."

Janice snorted. "Well I remember my dearly departed Bagston was in charge of this church and he got up there every Sunday with a little cocaine snort and the smell of his latest hussy on his body. Everybody seemed to put up with that!"

"Janice, we are so sorry you had to endure so much from your husband," sympathized Flo. "But we can't judge everyone in church by what he did. Most folks are very sincere in their beliefs."

"Well, Flo, I've got no quarrel with that, though I don't know how anyone here can be a judge of other's sincerity. You sure didn't see through Bagston. All I'm saying is you've already had a blasphemous devil as your preacher for all these years, what's wrong with a woman?"

Charley remembered he was in charge. "Calm down, Janice. We're not the enemy here. We all want to be fair and hear each other out. If we let our feelings control us here, we won't get anything done."

Jeanine added, "Remember, Janice, we didn't come to church to worship Bagston, but to worship God."

"That's not the way it looked to me, everybody fawning over him all the time! But I'll shut up about that if I can."

"Thank you, Janice. We appreciate that." Charley continued, "Now, does anyone have a recommendation about who to invite to preach? And how are we going to handle the finances? Do we need to elect a finance committee to handle the money? We don't want anyone to think that we are mishandling funds. There's been enough of that lately."

Ted decided to press the gender issue. "Good questions, Charley! But before we go there I'd just like to say that I think you have a point, Janice. What is wrong with having a woman? After all, we are not a selection committee for a pastor for our church. We are focusing on an event, a preach-off. Now I know we need to stay in certain bounds, but I think this is going to be big! It might even be an interfaith endeavor."

Flo agreed with Ted. "Maybe we could just throw out some names. I'm sure each of us has someone in mind. Otherwise, we wouldn't have such strong opinions. And we do have to consider the names that people in the congregation will submit. I was also thinking that we could leave open some time at the end of the week for those in the congregation who might want to speak."

Jeanine brightened. "Yes! I like that! It leaves some room for spirit working in folk. I vote for that."

Charley exhaled loudly. "Finally, something we can all agree on!"

"Charley, we got no room for feelings here," teased Janice.

All fell into laughing and sat back in their chairs. A more relaxed attitude entered and lounged around the room.

"Y'all might think this odd since I'm kind of known as THE LIBERAL around here but I submit the name of Little Jimmie Gallup. He's a bit of a buffoon in my view, but that boy can sure preach and he's got quite a following."

"You might have something there, Ted," said Flo. "Seems like I keep agreeing with you. Little Jimmie sure would be one to draw a crowd."

"Well, Flo, you agree with me because you are so smart."

Flo laughed "Ted, you are so modest."

Big grins all around.

Charley said invitingly, "We need somebody to write some of this down. We have one name to start the invitation list. Anyone volunteer to be the scribe?"

"I'll be happy to." Jeanine leaped in to be of service. "Unless someone else wants the job."

All gave their reassurances simultaneously. "No, no, you'd be good, Jeanine!"

"Are there any other recommendations for invitees?" Charley was getting into this chairing business.

"Ted, you might be good as one of the speakers." Jeanine couldn't believe she was saying that. After all, Ted was a self-proclaimed liberal. But he was a good speaker and had the best interests of the town at heart.

Ted was visibly touched. "Why thank you, Jeanine. I would be honored. I love this church and all the people in it. I'd try real hard not to color too far outside the lines, that is, if others think that my entry would be alright."

A chorus of assent. "It's a wonderful idea!" "Yeah, Ted, you'd be a good one."

Janice sniped, "That would be a refreshing change of pace after Bagston."

Flo placed her hand gently on Janice's shoulder. "Janice, don't go there again."

"Any other suggestions?"

"What about some of the well-known preachers? Like Charles Stanley or Joel Osteen. Do you think they would come?" Janice was getting enthused.

Flo responded, "I think we ought to invite them. Then it would be up to them. How about T. D. Jakes too?"

Janice just had to get in her opinion. "He would draw a big crowd. Can our choir handle all the music for this? Should we suggest that some of these preachers bring their own musicians? Miss Mary Jo is good on the organ, but she can't play that style of music."

Ted chuckled, his twelve-year-old was coming out. "Yeah, can you just see Miss Mary Jo trying to keep up with some of that contemporary music? She'd faint."

All laughed compassionately at the thought of Miss Mary Jo having to rouse herself out of her 2/4 tempo.

Janice had further inspiration. "Maybe we could issue an invitation to the Mighty River Flowing Gospel Singing Band. They can play most anything and keep up with anybody. And if the "big names" come they won't have to worry about a backup group. Everybody loves the Mighty River Flowing. It's about time we got some musicians to play some music that won't put everyone to sleep."

Ted was amazed and pleased at the transformation in this formerly dour and somewhat sour preacher's wife. "I love your spirit, Janice. It's like you are coming alive!"

"Alive is good, but let's not turn our church into a dance hall." Jeanine yelped."

Flo burst out laughing. "Dance hall? Jeanine, that conjures up some images! I don't think a preach-off is anywhere close to that!"

"Well, I think we should keep in mind that we are a church. We don't want people to get the wrong idea about us."

Ted leaped at this opportunity. "Have you ever heard of Sarah's circle? Quite the opposite of Jacob's ladder where everything is hierarchical and straight and 'proper.' Jesus invited his disciples to stand in a circle and they began dancing and singing and praising God."

"Ted! You know what I mean. You just have to get in your comments pushing your liberal views."

Jeanine's response was like throwing kerosene on Ted's fire. "Then there's King David dancing in the streets praising God. His wife leaned out the window with scorn and yelled at him to stop and be 'proper.' David never went in to her bedroom again. Wups! I alluded to sex."

"Ted, you're just trying to get my goat aren't you? You know the founders of our church would roll over in their graves if they knew such whooping and hollering was going on here."

"I thought the founder of our church was Jesus."

Much sighing, rolling of eyes, as well as smiles from the group.

Flo interjected, "I hate to change the subject, or maybe I don't. I heard a couple of ladies in the store talking about Mayhew's mob knowing about our plans for a preach-off. You know, I think someone in this town is letting them know what's going on. Should we try to take some precautions? What could we do?"

"I think you are pointing to a real concern there, Flo," said Charley. "I don't know if you want to go this far, but Luther knows some good old boys that are experienced in providing security …."

Janice trembled. "Do you think this is necessary? You're kinda making me scared."

"I understand, Janice. There is reason to be scared."

Jeanine snorted. "Charley, you mean those biker outlaws that Luther hangs out with? The ones that have provided security for those rock bands, those abominations of Satan?"

"Jeanine, those abominations may be just what we need to go up against Mayhew's group. The members of your Sunday School class just wouldn't do much good."

Everyone laughed. Jeanine's face reddened.

Flo said gently, "We aren't laughing at you, Jeanine. We may need professional help here. I suppose we could hire off duty police officers."

Ted sobered up from his foray into Jeanine's metaphysical jungle. "I think we are getting way off track here. What we are discussing is important and needs to be addressed but we are the credentials committee. Who are we reporting to anyway? Anyone? I suppose if we decide that we are in charge of the whole event we could do so."

Janice ignored Ted. "You folks just don't know what you're getting into with Mayhew. The more I learn about Bagston's dealings with him, the more I'm afraid. I think we should get any kind of security we can."

Charley took control. "Okay. What do you think about Ted's comment?"

A common chorus. "Ted's right". "We make the decisions." "Let's go for it."

Ted burst out laughing. "Yeaaa! Revolution!"

Flo looked at him. "Ted, do you need a break?"

"Flo, why don't you give me one?"

Flo laughed. "Okay, Ted. You win."

Charley grinned. "Let's get back to the meeting, please. Okay, we decided to invite outside music and get some kind of security. The good thing about asking Luther's friends is that they wouldn't expect payment."

Jeanine blew air through her nose. "No payment, hah! Beer and whatever else they might have their eyes on."

"Jeanine! Don't let your imagination run wild. Things aren't always like they are in those romance novels you like to read." said Flo.

Jeanine was a little embarrassed that her reading habits were a matter of public knowledge.

Charley announced, "It's getting late. Some of us may need to go. Let me summarize. We have named a few famous preachers that we will invite. As we get suggestions from the congregation, we will extend invitations to others. They may respond, and they may not. We can look over those that want to come. We have musicians in mind. Someone needs to contact them to see if they are available. I will talk to Luther about security." He laughed. "At least we will get him in church."

Flo looked at Jeanine. "I'll contact the musicians. Jeanine, will you help me with this?"

"Thank you, Flo." Jeanine cut her eyes at Ted. "I will even though it says in Leviticus to not consort with dancing fools."

Ted rises to the challenge. "Thanks, Jeanine. Guess you've seen me dance, huh?"

Charley couldn't resist taking up for his buddy. "And I heard Ted say once that it is better to be a fool than aloof."

Jeanine and Flo just sat shaking their heads. Janice giggled, beginning to feel a lot more comfortable as part of this group.

Charley tried once again to bring the meeting to a close. "The only other things I can think of would be the issue of parking, and seating. Can anyone else think of anything?"

Jeanine and Janice said simultaneously, "Food!"

"I knew if we gave you ladies long enough you'd find some way to have food served. How would you want to handle this? Like one of our homecomings?"

Janice said, "Actually Charley, I meant food NOW! We've been sitting here so long that I'm hungry. Anyone else?"

"Well, I'm adding food for the event to our agenda. Let's call it a night. Okay folks?"

"YES!"

Ted got bold. "Anyone want to join me over at the coffee shop?"

Jeanine said shyly, "I would, Ted."

Flo chuckled to herself, deciding not to take Ted up on his offer even though she was hungry. It was a way to pay Ted back for all his joking at her. She can just imagine Ted having to sit with Jeanine for the evening.

The others read the signs and bowed out.

Charley got up. "I'd like to join you, but I have something that I have to do."

Ted, a little miffed at Charley's abandoning him to Jeanine said, "Yeah, we know. Tell Millie we said hello."

All chuckled appreciatively

Charley blushed and called the meeting adjourned, then hastened out the door trying to maintain Baptist thoughts.

Jeanine and Ted

Jeanine and Ted were the only two that went to the coffee shop after the credentials committee meeting. Both were nervous. They hadn't been alone before and each considered the other as somewhat peculiar in the way they saw the world. They were of good heart, however, and welcomed each other's presence.

They made their opening moves. Jeanine said, "I haven't been in this coffee shop in a long time, Ted. I don't get out much except for church activities."

"Well, you should get out more, Jeanine."

She was a little flustered at Ted's directness. "Thanks, Ted, I guess I just get all caught up in the church and don't think about much else."

"Do you think the church is all there is to think about?"

"Yes, well......it's the most important thing to think about. There's the church and then there's the world. I certainly don't want to get caught up in worldly things."

"I see the whole world as church."

Jeanine groaned audibly. "Ted, that's just what I thought you would say. That remark is dangerously close to the devil's voice."

Ted laughed. "I'm sorry, Jeanine. I don't mean to make fun of your beliefs. But comparing my voice to the devil's is amusing. However, you're not the first one to feel that way. That's why I don't spend much time trying to convince anyone of how I see things."

"I don't want you to try to convince me of anything but I do want to know how you feel and think. You are a puzzle to me. You are such a goodhearted man and obviously sincere, but sometimes I wonder if you are a Christian."

That remark made Ted chuckle. "I know what you mean, Jeanine. I'm certainly not orthodox in my beliefs. You know what orthodox means at its root ? One who thinks straight down the party line. But that's not for me. I guess I just can't wear a straight jacket."

Fran, a waitress at the coffee shop, had been watching the pair since they came in. Ted and Jeanine weren't at her table, but she sure wanted to be the one to wait on them. Maybe she could get some idea of what they were talking about.

Fran sidled up to the table. "Can I get you two something?"

"I'm going to have coffee. What would you like, Jeanine?"

"Maybe a diet soda would be good."

"That's all? Be back in a minute." Fran was disappointed that she couldn't think of some reason to stand around. Listening to this unlikely pair would make for good gossip.

"Does that make sense what I said, Jeanine?"

"That you don't wear strait jackets?"

Ted smiled. "That I don't follow the conventional Baptist way of thinking."

"I knew what you meant. I was just trying to relieve the tension. I got to tell you, I feel more than a little uneasy talking with you. I know you are different in the way you see things. I just don't understand it. You are so regular at church and so helpful. Why do you come if you don't believe as the rest of us do?"

"We both love Jesus, don't we? No matter what the form of our belief."

Jeanine became a little irate. "Well, yes sir! I sure do believe in Jesus! Did you think for one minute that I didn't?"

"Whoo - weee! No wonder you didn't order coffee! You've got a hair trigger, Jeanine."

"Well, I'm sorry, Ted. I just get kinda angry at folks that don't think I'm a Christian. I have spent most of my life trying to prove that I am."

"I don't know anybody that would even have an inkling of a thought that you are not a Christian, Jeanine. In fact I heard someone say you are the only real Christian around. What happened to you that makes you think you have to prove it? How did you grow up anyway?"

"That's kinda personal. Let's just say that I had a real strict upbringing."

"I grew up in a strict home myself. We went to church every time the doors were open and we even invented reasons for opening the doors."

Jeanine laughed. "You must have had parents like mine. Only a trip to the emergency room or the undertaker would keep you out of church."

"Yes, the emergency room was really the only way out. The undertaker would wheel your body into the church for viewing."

Jeanine sat back in her chair now as she reached up to straighten her hair. She felt a little more at ease and a lot embarrassed that she had snapped at Ted.

Ted saw Jeanine straightening her hair and knew from his communication studies that it was a semi-flirtatious gesture. *Be careful here, old boy.*

Jeanine began to see Ted in a whole new light. Maybe he wasn't so bad after all.

"Ted, tell me a little about your beliefs. And break me in slowly. I don't want to attack you again."

"Okay, but feel free to respond however you need to. I know your heart is good."

He thinks my heart is good. Hmmm.... I wonder where this could lead. Jeanine thought. *Now, Jeanine, get a hold of yourself. This is Ted we're talking about.*

Ted saw Jeanine lick her lips and run her hands over her ample breasts and almost choked on his coffee. He thought he better shift this to more of an intellectual level.

"Okay, I'll tell you how I got to thinking the way I think." He saw her eyes begin to glaze over. "Don't worry. I'll give you the short version. I began to understand that every Christian on earth had a different understanding of who Jesus is and what Christianity is all about. Some of course had similar understandings and banded together. Every once in a while they would start to see things differently from each other and the band would break up, would split."

"So I began to understand that I would have to go my own way and not follow any band's doctrines. I left all the groups and began reading the Bible and researching the Bible's background -- who wrote what when -- and the background of Christianity and how it formed and changed over the years and decades and centuries."

"And I prayed and meditated and listened. After a while I realized that, at least for me, this little Baptist church and its people were closer to the heart and love of Jesus than any other place I knew. Even though I think a lot differently about the church and Christianity than most others, heart and love are the most important."

Jeanine looked perturbed. "I don't understand about Christianity changing over the years. The Bible doesn't change and God doesn't change. That's the only thing to believe in.

And the only way anyone could look at Jesus is that He is God's Son. Nothing else."

Ted said, "I respect your beliefs Jeanine."

"But ?"

"No but about it. I respect your beliefs."

Jeanine was thrown off balance. She expected resistance, not acceptance. "I just thought there was something else coming after that statement. Anyway, it's not just my beliefs. It's what the Bible says."

"Okay. Want some more diet soda?"

"No, thanks. I know there are a lot of people who call themselves Christians and wear it like some kind of badge. They go around bullying people. And actually they don't know anything about Jesus or God. Saying you are a Christian doesn't make you one. Anymore than saying you're a millionaire. It takes a personal relationship with God and His son. The show-offs are just like the Pharisees."

"I don't think you are a showoff, Jeanine."

"I wasn't talking about me! There you go again, Ted. Just as I start to feel like I can talk to you. I listened to you, didn't I?"

"I beg your pardon. Try again. Can you be a little more direct with me about what are you saying?"

"How can I be more direct? You either believe Jesus is God's son or you don't. You believe the Bible is God's word or not. Those who pretend to believe it and don't have done a lot of harm to others. And they make people not want to come to church. Most anybody can see through their put-on ways."

Ted responded gently. "I think this is what you want to know. We are the only two people sitting at this table. There is no *them* here. I believe that Jesus is God's son and you are God's daughter and I am God's son. We are children of the living God."

"I'm sorry, Ted. Guess I've been treating you like the enemy. I get carried away sometimes. I just get to thinking about Bagston and how he fooled people. I'm afraid he did a lot of harm to people here. Please be patient with me. I want to understand, but it's hard for me."

"Well, if I may continue to speak frankly, you certainly have some trigger points. Its like you are defending something even when it's not being attacked. And I see it starting to happen again right now. I'm not attacking you, Jeanine. I'm just saying what I think and I like it when you do the same."

"I guess I came in here prepared to defend my faith. I'm as bad as *them*. I haven't really been listening to you."

"I greatly appreciate your willingness to come into the lion's den."

Jeanine laughed. "You're more like an old bear, Ted."

"You have been listening, Jeanine. You see right through me."

"I wouldn't exactly say that. But I do have a different attitude about you than I did when we came in here."

"In that case, want to pick up the check?"

"Not a chance. Good try though. Seriously, since we have cleared the air some and broken down some barriers, maybe we could get together and talk again sometime."

"That would be fine."

"Sure. And I promise to leave my battle gear at home."

"Okay. Do you need a ride home? I don't have a car but I could call a taxi for you."

"No thanks. I think I'll walk. You have given me a lot to think about."

"Okay. Good night."

"Good night."

Bagston's Office

Janice unlocked the door to the office of her deceased-but-not-mourned-for husband. His engraved nameplate was still on the door: Reverend Milton T. Bagston. "I try to stay out of here. Too many bad memories. Besides he never wanted anyone in here anyway. Baggie always kept the door locked when he wasn't around."

Viola said, "Janice, is it alright that we look at everything in here? Keep in mind that some things might be more than disturbing to you."

"I can't get any more disturbed than I already am and have been. Feel free to look at everything. That's why we are here. I don't know all my husband was involved in, but we need to know it all."

"You need to know that if we find evidence of criminal activity, we will have to turn it over to the police. But from some of the things you have said, it seems that you don't mind if Bagston is exposed."

Janice said bitterly, "I think he exposed himself a lot already. Yes, I want to know the behind-the-scenes Bagston. I think it will help our church."

"Okay, where's a good place to start?"

"I have the keys to his filing cabinet. Let's look there first." Janice opened the cabinet and looked in the first drawer. "Oh, my God! Look at the balance on this bank account! I didn't even know he had this kind of money!"

Viola took a look. "It's unusual for anyone receiving funds illegally or as a bribe or anything of that nature to keep it where it is a matter of public record. We can easily find out whether he was depositing cash or check or so on. Or maybe someone wired the funds directly to his account. Janice, do you know where he might get this kind of money?"

"I have no idea! The money was in a bank in Atlanta, according to this paper. The only people he would have known there would be that Marlon Mayhew or someone who worked for him. I don't think any of his floozies would have given him that kind of money."

Viola mused, "It is just like Bagston to think he didn't have to hide anything. He had people so fooled here. He just thought no one would suspect him of anything wrong. Janice, let's take this a drawer at a time. No telling what we might find."

"You're right, Viola. He probably told Shoot Jennings down at the bank most anything and Shoot wouldn't have questioned him. Those boys were tighter than ticks on a hound.

Oh! Oh! Look at this! I've been so blind. Why didn't I see this happening?"

"What are you talking about, Janice?"

"That slimy little Thelma! Why didn't I see that she was involved with Bagston. Well, why not? He hardly missed any available pair of panties!"

Viola had been looking around Bagston's computer. "Is this her? I found this photo taped beneath the keyboard of this computer." She held up a photo of a semi-naked woman in a suggestive posture.

"O god, yes! That must have been taken years ago. She sure don't look like that now, but I recognize that face."

"What did you find in the file cabinet about her, Janice?"

"Some records of deposit to her from Bagston. It's been going on a long time. But why in the world would he be paying her?"

"Let me take a look at that. These are fairly substantial amounts. I don't think it would be for physical favors. Can you tell from looking at the account where the money came from?"

"My husband was both dumb and cocky. This account requires two signatures. Look who the other one is."

"Why it's that mob boss, Mayhew! You were right, Janice. Bagston did have ties to the mob. But what did Thelma have to do with it?"

The two continued to look painstakingly through mounds of records, finding more evidence of Bagston's gambling and whoring habits. Janice moved over to a lockbox in the corner, only to find more bank deposit statements.

As Viola reached way into the back of the bottom filing drawer, she found something that caused her to almost shout out.

She contained herself and tried to hide the document from Janice.

Janice snatched it from her. As she read it, she almost fainted.

It was a very old birth certificate from a hospital in Atlanta, a record of the birth of a girl born to Bagston.

Viola knew that Janice and Bagston had no children. The mother on the birth certificate was Flo and the baby was Millie!

Viola and Thelma

Viola arrived at her office early as was usually her practice. For this occasion, a session with Thelma, she especially wanted to be prepared. When she called Thelma and invited her to come over for a talk, Thelma had seemed neither surprised nor resistant. It was as if Thelma had expected Viola's invitation.

As a spiritual criminologist, Viola had made sure she received training in an understanding of all the world's religions and belief systems. *I will certainly need my knowledge in dealing with Thelma today,* she thought.

The door bell rang.

"Come in Thelma," said Viola. "It's good to see you."

Thelma thought Viola sounded kinda strange. "Why do you say that? Don't I usually come on this day? Is there something special going on?"

Viola wanted to put Thelma at ease. Otherwise she wouldn't get much out of her. "Why yes there is. Instead of our usual way of doing things and letting you take the lead on what we focus on, I've got something I really need to talk about with you today."

"Well then...shoot. I ain't got a whole lot on my mind anyway." Thelma was from the South, but she was not in any stretch of the imagination a southern lady. She seldom thought about what she was saying. She just opened her mouth and let the words fly.

"Thelma, this has to do with Reverend Bagston."

Thelma sat up in her chair. "Why in the world do you want to talk about that old heathen?"

"Janice asked me to help her look through some of his things the other day and we found some papers in his files concerning you."

"Me? What makes you think I had anything to do with him?" Thelma's tone of voice told Viola that she was definitely covering up something.

Viola continued, "The papers were a record of bank deposits in your account to your name. The deposits were pretty regular and from any standards quite a hefty sum."

"Lord, Viola. You sound like one of those old biddies down at the church. You're just making up a bunch of stuff. Where are those papers? I don't believe you found nothing!"

"Here, Thelma take a look."

Thelma quickly glanced at the papers. "So? This don't prove nothing."

"Why would Preacher Bagston give you this money every month and keep it secret? Thelma, what was going on?"

"That ain't none of your business! You keep this stuff up and I'm going home." Thelma was mad now and ready to make good her threat.

"Well, Thelma, if that is your attitude you are really going to need this!" (Viola pulled a chicken foot voodoo fetish out of her drawer and tossed it in Thelma's lap.)

Thelma screamed, jumped up and started mumbling some Cajun words that Viola couldn't understand. "Okay! Okay! I'll tell you anything you want to know. Just take this curse off of me!"

Viola had been aware of Thelma's Louisiana roots and how superstitious she was. Thelma's voodoo beliefs were always a source of laughter to the town folk. But Thelma took these things seriously.

"I'm sorry you take it as a curse, Thelma. Hand me the juju."

"I ain't touching that thing!" Thelma had gotten as far as she could into the corner of the room while constantly keeping her eye on the fetish.

"You take thet, you take thet thing Viola!"

Viola picked up the chicken foot from the floor. "Sit back down, Thelma, I've got it."

"I ain't sitting until you swear you'll take the curse off of me."

Viola saw she had Thelma right where she wanted her. "I will when you tell me what I want to know. Now, sit and start talking."

"Ok, ok. Bagston and I were what you might call dating for quite some time. He met me in Atlanta when I was a stripper."

"How long ago are you talking about?"

"Viola, I don't rightly know. It was several years ago before I came here and married Junior."

"That long? That means Bagston was seeing you for many years. No one here seemed to know about it."

"Yeah, he used to brag about how he had folks here fooled. I was a lot younger then. He kinda lost interest in me after......" Thelma suddenly stopped talking and looked as though she was about to burst into tears.

"After what, Thelma? What is it that bothers you so?"

"I ain't gonna tell you no more, Viola. And you can't make me neither."

Viola held the chicken foot as if she was going to toss it at Thelma again and began singing "Black Magic Woman."

"Stop it! Stop it! Viola, That's mean! Okay, I'll tell you. That old bastard got me knocked up."

"Oh, Thelma, I am so sorry. What happened to the baby? When you came here you had no child. Did you give it up for adoption?"

"There warn't no baby. He made me get rid of it." Thelma slumped down in her chair and started sobbing uncontrollably.

Viola put the chicken foot away and sat quietly by Thelma. "You had an abortion?"

"Yes, and I've wished a thousand times that I hadn't of. But Bagston was so afraid of losing his almighty position that he said I had to. If'n I didn't he'd tell Mayhew about me. I'd lose my job. I didn't have no one to take care of me then. You understand, Viola, don't you?"

"Yes, I do. You have been through a lot of suffering and are still going through it. Is that what this money that Bagston gave you every month is all about?"

"Yeah! But, I weren't as dumb as he thought I was. I swore to myself I'd make him pay. So, I asked the doctor that performed the abortion to save me a little piece of my baby. I heard that some people were doing that when their babies was born. Then I took it to a cop I knew and he had that DNA testing done to it."

"So you had that half of the proof that Bagston was the father. How about the other half?"

"It warn't no trouble at all. I just had to make Bagston think I still wanted him. His old horny ways made it easy for me to get a sample of his spit. My cop friend told me what to do."

Viola sighed, knowing the rest of the story but needing to hear it from Thelma's lips. "So then what did you do?"

"Well, when I had it in writin' that Bagston was the daddy of my poor little baby, I showed the paper to him. I told him he was gonna pay and pay big."

"What was his reaction?" Viola could only imagine what Bagston might have done.

"He slammed me around some. Then he tore up the papers. I just laughed and told him the real copy was with my cop friend. I finally had that ol' slime exactly where I wanted him! Then I explained to him that he would have to come up with some money for me to keep my mouth shut."

Viola held up the papers she had shown Thelma. "So that's what these bank records are -- hush money?"

"Yep. And you can see it cost him big time. The money was what kept me and Junior going. While I'm telling you all this, I guess I'd better tell you the whole thing. You ain't gonna get that chick'n foot out again, are you?"

Viola ignored the chicken foot question. "You've come this far. You may as well tell me everything now." She thought if what she had already heard wasn't the whole thing she wasn't sure she wanted to hear the rest.

"Well, when Mayhew found out I left Atlanta to come here, he just wadn't gonna let me go. And I was so mad at Bagston that I agreed to keep Mayhew up on everything Bagston was doing here."

"What does that mean, Thelma?"

"Well, I guess you could say I was a spy for the mob. What do they call it?... a gopher or something."

Viola laughed to herself but kept a straight face. "A mole, Thelma."

"Oh yeah, I just don't know all them technical words. Anyway, Mayhew said he'd let me go if I'd let him know everything Bagston did. Bagston was into it pretty heavy with the mob. They was planning on taking over this town somehow. But they never told me anything about it."

"Are there any specifics that you know? Anything you remember would help. You know we are trying to save our church. The more we know the better."

Thelma thought a minute. "I know that Bagston was pretty heavy in debt to Mayhew over some gamblin'. I heard that old faker was gonna turn over the church bonds and deeds to Mayhew to help pay him back."

"Thank you, Thelma. I know this has been draining today for both of us, but especially for you. Let's end our meeting now. Can we sit quietly for a moment while I ask for goodness for you?"

Tears ran down Thelma's face. "Miss Viola, do you really think I deserve any goodness? 'Specially after what all I just told you?"

"We all have messed up in our lives, Thelma. Every single one of us. There is a Bible verse I like -- 'If we confess our sins, He is faithful and just to forgive us our sins.' You just confessed a lot, and you will get just as much forgiveness."

"Miss Viola, you're a saint! You be careful though. I've seen a couple of Mayhew's men around town lately."

"I'm far from a saint, but thank you. Would one of those be a man named Freddy?"

Thelma seemed surprised that Viola knew that name. "Sure is! He's one of the meanest. He's so mean they say he's the best friend of a demon."

Viola thought to herself, *Gregor.*

Viola put her arm around Thelma. "Ok. Let's sit quietly for a while. I will pray for goodness to open even more in your heart and for all evil to be kept from you."

Little Jimmie Gallup

Little Jimmie Gallup visited his hair stylist every Saturday, in preparation for Sunday's televised "The Little Jimmie Gallup Gospel Hour" where he would prance and cavort, gyrate and leap, spin and twirl on the stage before the Lord and his worshipping admirers. Jimmie Gallup's worshipping admirers, not the Lord's.

He sighed. He gave so much to others! The unwashed mob, as he privately called them, did not even begin to know the sacrifice necessary to give them what they needed and demanded!

He had to stay in shape. He had to wear white suits. He had to resist the temptation of the women and young girls who threw themselves his way (which he had pretty much done, except for three or four or so times). And that damned collar he had designed for himself (at the same time he had anointed himself as a Bishop of the Church of the Everlasting Seeking) chafed his neck.

I *really must redesign my preaching outfit,* he thought.

Fortunately he would be going on a road tour soon. And that would take him through the Deep South where preachers were regarded in high esteem who took off their coats, their ties and collars, as they sweated and jumped and cavorted.

Jimmie loved that word. He regarded himself as a Master of Cavort.

Jimmie was practiced at regarding himself. He was always checking himself out in the mirror of his mind. He loved what he saw.

At the moment, he was looking into an actual mirror, the one the hair stylist held before him. "Looking good!" said Gallup as he turned his head and preened.

"Where are you headed to this time, Jimmie?"

"Oh, some little town in Georgia, some little church where the minister just died. They are looking for a lifting of their spirits, a true revival."

"Well, you are just the man who can give it to them, Jimmie!" Little Jimmie Gallup rose from the chair. "And Jimmie, don't forget! If you want your hair to be in good shape tomorrow, sleep with a pair of silk panties on your head."

Gallup laughed. It was a standing joke between the two. He actually followed the hair stylist's advice. He had a pretty good selection of panties to choose from.

To: The Subliminal Sublime

To: The Subliminal Sublime, the Underpinning, the Supreme Sublation, the Ground Floor and the Overhead

From: The Angel of Fire
Subject: Charisma
Our Holiness,

The humans are truly a strange and marvelous bunch. Some of them have already opened their consciousness to the actual world they live in – this world infinitely spiraling from the subatomic to the metagalactic, infinity in all "directions" – while others are still living in feudal existence thinking you are "out there" somewhere "above" and must be placated, worshipped, adored. The latter do not realize (it is not "real" to them) that what their religions have called for (eternal open existence in continuous communication with you and all existing) has happened. They are still caught in an old mode of thinking from a previous world, where the sun "rises" and "sets," where they believe they are separate beings. They have not awakened to the realization that they are interwhirlings of an infinite cosmos.

I am most interested in reporting my observations on the peculiar phenomenon that humans fall prey to called charisma. This is their name for the energies that radiate from a person who has liberated himself from existing thought forms. S/he is free from conventional morality and thus radiates a confidence not affected by guilt or the usual fears and anxieties that conventional morality induces. People who feel trapped are attracted to such radiance.

Unfortunately, many humans are blinded by another's charisma or radiance, not able to tell whether the confidence is a "con" or is true through and through. Those who have not opened to their own radiance want to set the radiant one up as a leader to be followed unquestioningly. In effect, they con themselves.

This is what has happened in the Baptist church we are observing so closely. Their minister, Bagston, exuded confidence so strongly that even those with some suspicions cast the blame upon themselves, praying piteously for forgiveness for their evil thoughts toward a man of God. Bagston preyed on this self-abnegation without mercy.

Humans tend to ignore the understanding that charisma exists only in relationship – as a two-way street. Just as the cursor arrow on a computer screen is useless without something to click on, so Bagston's "charisma" would have been fruitless if the folk had not been so needy and so gullible. There is no use telling most of them that, however. They prefer to feel indignant and victimized rather than to claim their own power. The situation they are in was brought on by themselves.

O well. They are where they are. They are looking to solve their dilemma now by more of the same. They are getting set to invite people with charisma to come and entertain them and pump them up. At the same time, they hope to make enough money (a fictional god but one they all believe in) to pay off the debts Bagston produced by, in effect, selling the church behind the member's backs, as some would claim, but from my point of view, right in front of their faces.

Whether they realize it or not, these humans are continuing to buy into the game of church. The positive outcome of it is that people who would ordinarily not be seen in each other's presence are working together with a common goal. Not exactly what Yeshua intended when he paid a visit to this planet, but that is another story. A story which you, Our Holiness, already know.

I of course will remain here until I complete my mission. Further reports to be forwarded to you and the Planetary Council as necessary.

Blessings to all on the Council
and to all everywhere.

P. S. Gregor is growing in understanding and may even be included in the Charismatic Preach-Off. You were right about him. I lose the bet.

Thelma Tells All to Junior

As Thelma pulled her jeep into her driveway, she saw Junior sprawled out on his hammock on the front porch. What was she going to tell him?

Did she have to tell him anything at all? Having confessed all to Viola she felt a sense of relief. Could Junior be as understanding?

From all appearances most folks thought that Thelma didn't care much for Junior. It was a strange relationship they had. She was a lot more than bossy to him, and he took it. Thelma couldn't even remember now how they came to this. Guess they had started off this way.

Thelma was born in a little bayou town in Louisiana. Her folks moved here when she started high school. That's where she met Junior. They were a hot item for several years until Thelma got bored and took off for Atlanta to see what life really had to offer her. That's when she got caught up with Mayhew. He had promised Thelma a career in show business. Oh, it was 'show' business alright... stripping every night in that club full of howling men.

What Thelma thought was the high life had turned into a living hell for her. Her only value to anyone was when she stripped in front of them and let them paw all over her. That's how she got involved with Bagston. He would come to the club, hooting and hollering just like the rest of those men. Then he would find a way to spend some time with Thelma. He knew just how to talk to Thelma and say all the things she needed to hear. She thought he really cared about her, but time sure proved her wrong. Thelma did a lot of growing up the hard way.

After having to give up her precious baby, she couldn't stay in that filthy club. She thought of Junior and the small town where she had lived. So, she packed up and went back. Junior took her back without question. Guess that's what real love is all about. But everyone else looked down on her. Every town, church, neighborhood has its pecking order. And Thelma was the lowest of the low. But not to Junior. She was his queen, but she didn't exactly allow him to be the king of his castle. Life in Atlanta had made her hard. And she took it out on Junior. Guess that's how we treat those who love us sometimes.

Thelma thought of all the mean things she had said about Millie. Most of it was because she was afraid someone would find out about her relationship with Bagston and she would be accused of murdering him. She was so wrong to talk about Millie that way.

Looking at Junior now, asleep in that hammock, she felt remorse for how she had treated him. It came over her so strong she could hardly breathe. She loved that man. How could she have treated him so badly?

And why had he put up with it? She began to cry again. What if she told Junior about the baby and he left her? This could be the one thing he wouldn't take. Well, it was too late now. That escaping horse had left the barn door wide open and it couldn't be shut now.

Coming up the front steps onto the porch, Thelma softly called his name… "Junior." He looked so peaceful lying there. It almost broke her heart to wake him up out of that peaceful sleep. What she had to tell him just might be the last peace either one of them felt for awhile. "Junior", she called again as she stroked his hair back from his forehead.

"Yeah, what do you want, Thelma? Where have you been? You don't usually stay so long with Viola." Junior saw something in Thelma's eyes that made him jump right up. "What's wrong. Did somebody die?"

"Well yes Junior, but not anybody you knew. Come inside and I'll tell you about it."

That afternoon seemed like an eternity to Thelma. She told Junior all about her time in Atlanta, her thing with Bagston, and then her precious baby she had to give up. He listened without saying a word. When she finished, he stood up and held her tighter but softer than she had ever known. Both of them shed a lot of tears, but there was no judging, or 'why didn't you's. Just love. Thelma finally realized that she had here with Junior what she had been searching for.

Free-Flowing River

Charley and Luther walked along the shore of what was once a free-flowing river but had been dammed (*damned* was what Luther called it) by the Corpse of Engineers (another Lutherism).

"Look at that, Charley. It reminds me of all our belief systems that we get stuck in."

Charley looked. All he saw was a large placid lake. "You mean they are calming?"

Luther laughed. "Calming is it alright. If you think of calming as self-hypnosis."

He continued, "All doctrine, including that Baptist belief system you are stuck in, with all due respect, is dam-nation. It serves a purpose in one way in that it calms people's anxieties and fears. It's downside is that people think the safe little lake that is formed is the whole cosmos, that it is the one true reality, that anything that exists outside these shores is wrong and bad and evil. People don't bother to stop and think that their lake of belief was formed by putting bounds on the free-flowing river."

Charley started getting uncomfortable. Though Luther was his best friend, Charley didn't like it when Luther started questioning the very ground on which Charley stood (or from Luther's point of view thought he stood). He blurted out, "Luther, my Baptist doctrine as you call it is not a lake. It is the free-flowing river."

"That's what those fish out there think, Charley, if they bother to think at all. When you are immersed in the lake, you can only see from that perspective. I see you are taking this personally once again, Charley. I can tell by the look on your face. You have no problem thinking that what I am saying is true for all other doctrines, that those poor fish are caught in a dammed lake, consigned to dam-nation. But you have the arrogance to think that your doctrine is not a lake at all."

"Well, it's not, Luther! It's the truth!"

"Sounds a little fishy to me, Charley." said Luther, smiling. "If you had been born into another culture, a different family, you might be standing here defending the Koran as the only word of God and Islam as the only way. And it would be those Christians who have it all wrong."

"Luther, you have the dangdest way of looking at things. You remind me of one of those politicians. You can make things look just the way you want them to. I know there is no use in me quoting Scripture to you. You'll see it like it's a fish in the Dead Sea."

Both laughed.

"We do have some kind of conversations, don't we? But you are more right than you might realize when you say I remind you of politicians. Religion and politics are pretty much the same. Everybody has their story to tell and everybody wants you to believe it."

"What you don't know, Luther, is that we Christians are not worshipping the lake but the God who made the lake, oceans, fish and the whole shebang."

"Well, we are similar in that regard. I'd just change one word in what you just said 'making' instead of 'made.' I love the God who is making the whole he bang."

"There you go again, Luther. Hanging on to a word. You and I both know that God is still at work here. If he had created everything and then left man on his own, the world would be in a sorrier mess than it is now."

"Words make a difference, Charley. "Made" is past tense. So we have to say what we mean. There's another difference in what you believe and what I believe. You seem to believe that God is out there somewhere, separate from all this, but intervenes from time to time. I see all that is and God as not separate at all."

"Luther, you are putting Christians in a bag marked 'stupid.' Now there are some people who connect themselves with a church or a denomination and don't have a clue about who God is. But Christians who have taken the time to develop a relationship with God are not so narrow minded. God's not 'out there.' He's here." Charley points to himself.

"Exactly. God is not separate from us at all. Your Christian Holy Book tells us that He is in us and we are in Him. 'In whom we live and move and have our being.'"

Charley grins. "In theological language that is called panentheism."

"Whatever you want to call it. My Buddhist friends call it 'mutual co-arising.'"

"Luther, some people have a 'religion'. Those Baptistions, Lutherans, Presbyterians, or whatever are the ones who make you so annoyed. They bother me too.

We don't get to make up the rules. God has already done that. I don't think that you and I have really talked much to know what each other believes. We assume we do, but from things we've said, I don't think we do. I can't lump you with all 'heathens' and you can't lump me with all Pharisees."

"You are right, Charley. Which means I agree with you. As we hang out together and put up with each other, we get to know that the other one can't be put in any kind of box. Though I don't mind being called a heathen -- one from the heath and the heather -- and I have certainly never thought of you as a Pharisee."

"Well thanks, Luther. I'll take any compliment I can get from you."

"Well take this then, buddy!" Luther feinted a blow to Charley's head which he easily blocked.

"Since you're in such an agreeable mood, I need to ask a favor of you."

"What?"

"You ain't gonna like this much, because it has to do with church."

"No, I don't want to go."

"Just listen, Luther. This is a chance of a lifetime for you. I know you have heard of the Preach-Off we're gonna have at the church."

"Now you're talking. I would love to deliver a sermon."

Charley laughed. "I just bet you would. This is even better. How about you and your biker buddies going up against the mob?"

"The church mob? You want me to round up some guys and go up against the whole mob of you?"

Charley laughingly attempted to slap Luther up side his head. "No, though I know that would be a dream come true for you. We have found that the mob has their hooks into the finances of the church. They don't cotton to having their plans for taking over ruined. So, we need some security during the Preach-Off to see that no one gets hurt."

Luther easily blocked Charley's slap and twisted his wrist into a submission hold. "If I do get some buddies we would have to have free run of the place of course. And with frisking privileges."

"Is this so you can feel up our women folk?"

"Absolutely!"

"I was just kidding. Maybe we need some security to watch the security."

"Okay, I'll get serious. Because this is serious business, Charley. If you expect mob violence in any form it will have to be prevented if possible. And if not, force must be met with force. Is your church ready for that?"

"Probably not. Most of them don't have a clue what we're up against and wouldn't have the slightest idea what to do about it. That's why the committee chose you and your buddies. We will be dependent on you to do whatever is necessary to protect us."

"I'll give it some thought. I'll tell you this though, we won't be carrying any guns. They cause more trouble than they are worth. They are out of place at an event like yours anyway. I'll talk with some of the guys and see if they are open to this. Most of them have experience at providing security at rock concerts so they will probably be up for it."

"We don't know right now how much we can pay you. It depends on what is taken in during the meetings. Are you alright with that?"

"Just let us date your daughters and eat in your homes for an indefinite period of time."

"L-U-T-H-E-R!"

Luther laughed. "I don't often get the opportunity to play the heathen, especially one guarding the sanctity and decorum of the saved."

"You are hopeless! But thanks for doing this for us. Do you realize this will make the church indebted to you? That ought to be good for a few years of jokes for you."

"I'm looking forward to that! No firm promises right now except I'll talk with the others and see what they say . But I have a feeling they will really like this gig!"

"I kinda figured that." As Charley walked away, he thought, *Lord, help us. What have we gotten ourselves into?*

Luther headed down to look without fondness once again at the dam, hoping there might be some weaknesses in its structure. *That Charley! He doesn't know what he's gotten into this time!*

Viola Confronts Flo

With the information uncovered from the search of Bagston's study, Viola knew she would now have to confront Flo. The birth certificate found was evidence that Flo could have had a part in Bagston's murder. Viola knew she had to get to Flo before Janice did. Janice was like a time bomb about to blow. Venting her anger and hurt was more important to her right now than considering anyone's feelings. She would not be able to resist facing Flo.

Rather than just dropping in at Flo's house, which was still an accepted custom in this little southern town, Viola decided to make it a more formal visit by calling ahead and asking Flo if this was a good time for her to come over.

Flo seemed a little surprised, but told Viola to please come over. She would make some tea. Viola knew what that meant. Iced tea that when previously hot would be loaded with sugar. It was a pretty good drink for the hot muggy weather though. Perked a person up a bit.

Viola strolled over from her place and called through the screen door, "Flo, it's me, Viola!"

"Come on in, Viola. The door's not locked." Now folks in a small town like this one seldom locked their doors. If they did, it was thought that they had something to hide. Or had recently moved in from the north or some other place where folk didn't know the meaning of hospitality and always making oneself available for the visits and concerns of others.

"It's pretty hot out there, Viola. Can I pour you a glass of tea? Do you prefer lemon or mint?"

"Ummm!!! That mint sounds good, Flo! Thank you!" Most small-town southern folks kept mint growing outside their kitchen doors. It was handy when you needed it and it was always fresh.

As the two ladies sat down at the kitchen table, Flo couldn't wait any longer to find out the reason for Viola's visit. "What exactly did you want to see me about? You don't usually call before a visit."

Viola could see that Flo was on to her. "You are attuned to the nuances of things as usual, Flo. I appreciate your sensitivity (*and your toughness too*, she thought). I'm here both as me and in my profession as spiritual criminologist. That feels kind of awkward, visiting with you and at the same time having something else on my mind."

"I'm trying hard to understand what you're getting at, Viola. But you sound a little uptight about it. Can we just handle this as friends?" Flo was feeling more ill at ease with each moment.

"Friends we are and friends I hope we'll always be. I'm investigating something, Flo, and I hope you can shed some light on a few things."

"I'll be glad to share with you anything I know. Who's in trouble this time?" The impatience with Viola's not getting to the point was beginning to show in Flo's face.

"It has to do with Bagston's death. I was over at Janice's at her invitation going through some of the files and things in his home office."

Flo thought to herself, *Oh, my Lord. What have they found?*

Viola continued sipping on her cold frosty iced mint tea while noticing Flo's consternation. "We found a document with your name on it, Flo."

"Why in the world would my name be on anything in Bagston's office? Are you sure it was me?"

Viola once again picked up on some anxiety in Flo's voice. "Yes, I'll show you a copy of it in a moment and you can see if you can verify it. Let me ask you, what did you think of Bagston? Did you like him? Do you think he was a good man?"

"Do I need a lawyer?" Flo gave an uncomfortable laugh.

"Now Flo, you know I have no legal standing."

"Well, I don't see what difference it makes how I felt about that man. I don't think it's a secret that I didn't think too well of him. I never saw fit to step foot in his church for quite a few years. I saw him as a hypocrite. Is that what you're looking for?"

"I have reason to believe that Bagston did you wrong, Flo. That he treated you terribly. I know you are a tough, smart, strong woman and good at taking whatever life sends your way and dealing with it by yourself. But I think some things are about to become public knowledge now in spite of what I want. Or what you want, Flo."

Flo felt herself go flush with fear. She knew that the very thing she had tried to conceal was about to become common knowledge. It was a joy to her that Millie had come to realize that she was her mother. But for the whole town to know...that was more than she could bear. What would this do to her precious daughter? And....oh, oh.....was Viola thinking she had anything to do with Bagston's death? If she thought that Viola would believe it, she would certainly fake a swoon right now.

"Here is a copy of the document we found." Viola reached over and handed Flo a copy of Millie's birth certificate.

Flo's hand shook so badly that she could hardly read the document. She did recognize it as a birth certificate...Millie's birth certificate. And she and Bagston were listed as the parents! She couldn't speak for a few minutes. Finally the words came, "Viola, I beg you. If you consider me your friend at all, please don't show this to anyone! Or has someone else seen it already?"

"I'm afraid so, Flo. Janice has seen it. We were going through Bagston's documents together."

"Janice? No! There is no way she could ever understand the circumstances behind this. She'll be out for blood. Just how far has this gone, Viola?"

"Only this far for now. But it's going to go further, Flo. There is a suspected murder involved, and if that suspicion proves correct, there is possibly a murderer living here amongst us in our community."

"And you think it's me?" Flo jumped up and began to pace around the room. "I hated that man for sure. I thought of a thousand ways I would like to see him die. That sanctimonious monster! Living like such a saint and fooling the people around here just like he fooled me at one time. Then when I found out he had tried to push himself on Millie...his own daughter! And he knew she was his daughter! I guess I've said too much. I suppose it does look like I did it."

(Fierce knocking and blamming on the screen door, rattling it in it's frame) It was Janice, screaming at the top of her voice, "Let me in! Let me in, you bitch whore!"

"O, lord, Viola. It's Janice! I can't talk to her right now. What am I gonna do? Help me!"

"Just sit tight." Viola headed for the door and out onto the porch. "Janice! Calm down! What do you think you are doing?"

Janice didn't quiet down one bit. "I think I'm calling out that bitch who screwed around with my husband. That's what I think I'm doing! Is she in there? I know she is. Just wait until I get my hands on her!"

Viola took Janice by the shoulders, "Get your hands on her? You'll do no such thing. Get a hold of yourself. You've probably got everyone on the street peeking out their windows by now. Sit down over here on the porch swing." Janice sat but she didn't want to.

"Janice, think a minute. Flo was just a mere girl when this happened. She looked up to Bagston just like everyone else did. He probably convinced her that there was nothing wrong with what he did. You can't go in there now and try to punish her for what she did so many years ago. Besides, she decided to have the baby. And she cared enough about the baby's welfare to see that she was given to people who would love and care for her. Flo has lived in this town for awhile now. Does she strike you as a whore? Why she doesn't even date anyone. Think, Janice!"

Janice was soothed somewhat by Viola's voice and the porch swing with its rhythmic creaking as it swung. She heaved a big sigh, "I'm just so angry, Vi !"

"I know. And rightfully so. But don't take your anger out on someone who has been as much a victim as you."

Janice was once diagnosed as "having" a borderline personality disorder, primarily on her ability to become charged with emotion and then being able to turn on a dime into a charming schoolgirl. "You're right, Vi." Calling out to Flo in sweet intonations, "Flo! Flo, dear! I'm sorry!"

Viola patted Janice on the hand, thankful that she was able to calm down this tornado. "Do you think you can go in there now and talk civilly to her?"

Janice started to feel a little ashamed of her fit pitching. "I don't want to face her right now. I'll see if she wants to talk with me another time. Will you give her my apologies?"

"Yes, of course. Maybe it would be good if you two could talk when things have cooled down a bit. I'll come see you later. Would you like that?"

"Yes. Thank you Viola! You're the greatest!"

Watching Janice walk down the steps and into the street, Viola thought, *That poor woman. She's gonna need all the help she can get.*

Viola grabbed the screen door handle and called out, "Don't shoot, Flo. The coast is clear. I'm coming in alone."

Flo Tells Millie of Viola's Find

Flo had gone out the back door while Viola was dealing with Janice's frenzy. She knew she had to get to Millie before anyone else did. She could not bear to have Millie hurt once more by Bagston. And now the whole town would know. Janice had seen to that. By now, the phone lines were burning up with this latest bit of gossip.

How would she tell Millie? Would this cause Millie to shun her? How much more would they have to endure because of this monster Bagston? Flo was comforted by the knowledge that he was now getting his just rewards. She knew that much about the Bible. Bagston would eternally pay for what he had done. But why should so many innocent people have to pay? Flo was willing to accept her part in this, but what about poor Millie? She had just begun to grow and develop a life of her own. She had come to know the value of herself. The relationship with Charley was such a good thing for her.

Before Flo could think of another why or what if, she had reached the library where Millie was working. She tried to calm herself some before she entered so she would not scare Millie and alert everyone else that something was wrong. "Millie, do you have some time to take a walk with me?"

"Well, yes, Flo. Let me just check in this last book and I'll be right with you."

As the two women walked out into the pleasantness of the day, Flo's mind was racing.

"Flo, what's wrong? You seem so upset. Is there something I can help you with?"

"No, Millie. This is something I have gotten myself into, but I'm afraid it involves you."

"What in the world are you talking about? Here, let's sit down on this bench and talk about it. After all, I don't think there's anything we can't say to each other now, do you?"

"Millie, Janice Bagston has found your birth certificate in some files that Bagston had in his office! Viola has seen it, and I don't know how to protect you. Everyone is going to know." There. Flo had blurted it out without even taking a breath.

Millie just sat there and stared at Flo. She heard the words, but their meaning just didn't register with her. It took her a few minutes to take it all in.

"Millie, did you hear me? Please, say something."

"I don't quite know what to say. I have had some time to deal with the fact that Bagston was my dad. As bad as that is, the good part is that you are my mother. This was bound to come out sooner or later. People in this town have to have something to talk about. We don't know that someone hasn't figured it out already. We have each other, and I have Charley now. Besides, the Huckleberrys aren't going to stand for anyone causing either one of us trouble. Lordy, can you imagine what Luther would do?" Both laugh at that thought and share a loving hug. Flo looked at her bright, beautiful daughter and thought to herself what a strong woman she is growing into.

"Millie, you realize that I could be considered a suspect in Bagston's murder, don't you?"

"Well, that's just ridiculous. If it comes to that, we'll hire us a good lawyer. Don't worry, Mom. God's gonna get us through this."

Luther and Security

Charley was nervous. Two of the worlds in which he lived were about to collide. In his world of Christianity, he was cozily tucked away in the body of believers where he had his role and function as youth minister, young Christian on the rise, advancing toward sainthood, and not expected to fall into worldly ways. He knew that most of the church folk thought (if they thought at all) that he was sexless, unemotional, and his knees were scarred from praying. He knew that if he ever married, he would be expected to make love only in the missionary position and for the sole purpose of having babies.

And then there was the world according to Luther to which Charley had a passport and was on his way to becoming a citizen. In that world Charley was seen as a fledgling who had yet to fully test his wings. "You've gone to seed before you have even flowered," Luther would say. "Take off that strait-jacket and come on out here." With Luther, Charley had learned the power and sense of flowing energy of the martial arts and the ability to strike a blow as well as receive one. Luther enjoyed reminding him that Jesus said, "I did not come to bring peace, but a sword." Luther was a wild man, loving and kind, but also fierce and unpredictable. And now he was sitting here, waiting for Charley to call the Credentials Committee meeting to order!

Charley, his throat dry and his voice cracking, said, "Looks like we are all here. Shall we begin?"

Charley called the Credentials Committee to order. "Last meeting we all agreed we needed some kind of security at our preach-off. I have talked to Luther, that's why I invited him here.(Nodding a welcome to Luther) Luther has his own ideas about how security should be handled. I will let him tell you about it."

Luther stood and looked them over with his clear open gaze and his semi-mocking smile.

"I'm not sure you folks know what you are getting into with asking for security for this preach-off. You have some decisions to make. But first I need to ask you, why do you feel you need security? Aren't you folk supposed to live by faith?"

Jeanine leaped to answer for them all. "Yes, Luther, we do. But I think it would be foolish not to be prepared in case the mob tries to take over. They can be pretty violent."

Flo jumped in. "Luther, do you think we should do away with our police departments just because we live by faith?"

Ted groaned. "Let's not get all defensive and get into heavy theological discussions and Bible quoting here. We are talking about a simple fact. We want to provide some protection against the possibility of certain folk attempting to disrupt our trying to get the church out of hock."

"Ted's right." Charley was relieved at the opportunity to un-jib Luther's jibe. "We don't expect Luther and his friends to strong arm anyone. Just be there in case we need them."

Luther waded in. "That's what I'm trying to get clear. Who is this 'mob' you are referring to? I need some faces not some vague reference."

"The 'mob' we are talking about is a group of ruthless people who run the gambling business in Atlanta," explained Charley. "They own the night clubs, too. We don't know just how far reaching they are, but we do know they want their hands on our church property in order to set up one of their businesses here."

"Does anyone here know the members of this group? Not that we have to get into that right now. If you do know, then I can meet with one or two of you later for that info. If you don't know, I would recommend you talk with Viola Trumpett and get her on that right away. The first rule of the security business is know your enemy."

Janice volunteered. "I know one of them is that vile Marlin Mayhew. My not so dearly departed husband was a regular customer at his establishment."

"So Marlin is involved. I know who he is and some of his employees. Is that it? Just Marlin and his buddies?"

Charley answered for the group. "We think that's it for now. There is one person here in town that used to work for him. That's Thelma. We're not sure whether she is still involved with him or not. Anyway, Bagston's appetite for Marlin's place of business is how Marlin came to know about our town."

"Well, hell. Wups, excuse me (noticing Jeanine's face go red), if that's all you are worried about, I think we can do business. My friends and I can handle anything Marlin can dish out. That brings me to another point -- do you want us armed?"

Charley's face contorted at the thought of guns in church. "Do you think that's necessary, Luther?"

"No. But I need to ask. You are the ones doing the hiring. I don't know what your expectations are."

Janice said, "I'd like to see you blow them all away."

Luther saw something he recognized in Janice's eyes. "Janice dear, would you like to climb on my hog sometimes and go somewhere to shoot my pistol?"

Ted shook his head in disbelief. "Now take it easy, Luther. No call to get sarcastic. Janice has been through a lot because of these folks." Ted did not notice that Janice was more than open to Luther's suggestion.

"Okay, just funning around. Sorry, Janice." Janice looked at Luther with a small grin on her face. "What do the rest of you peace-loving folk think?"

Flo, who appreciated a good pistol, especially her Glock, said. "I don't think guns are necessary. Innocent people could get hurt."

"That's right," Jeanine chimed in. "All we really want to do is see that our preach-off goes on without interruption. If we can't earn the money, these people could take our church away from us."

"Okay, makes sense to me. Next question -- how tight do you want the security to be? Folk frisked at the door? Everyone wearing a name tag and registration badge which gives them entry? A machine everyone has to pass through? Or just a general eye on things and looking for any suspected troublemakers?"

Ted was pleased. "Luther, I've known you since you were a little boy. You might like to appear to be wild as a betsy bug, but you have a level head about you. We trust you to decide how it should be handled. We don't need nothing dramatic. Everyone agree?"

Jeanine, who often felt it her duty to correct the world and move it into a shape more her liking, said, "Ted, that was a double negative you used. You are usually more grammatically correct!" Ted shifted uneasily at this too intimate intrusion into his space. "Yes, I do. I agree that security should be hired to keep a general eye on things."

Flo looked questioningly at Jeanine as if she was someone she didn't even know. "I agree. After all, this is to be a church service."

Janice spoke in a sultry voice. "Luther, how much is this going to cost us?"

Luther could not have asked for a better opening. "Why you folk know the love of money is the root of all evil. I was telling Charley how about if me and my buddies date your women and eat meals in your homes for a time?"

Charley was aghast. "Luther!!!"

Ted and Flo laughed. Jeanine looked like she had just seen Satan himself. Janice looked like she wanted to make Luther's suggestion a motion.

"Charley said that since you don't know how much money you are going to take in, we could arrange that later. However, I have here a contract I would like this committee to look at and sign. There is a set amount I am asking and then a percentage of the gate if it goes beyond that bottom line fee."

Charley passeed around the contract and waited for everyone to look at it.

"Everyone in agreement?"

Ted said, "I don't see that we have a whole lot of choice. It wouldn't be fair to ask you to do this without pay. And we can't have this preach-off without security. So, I vote yes."

Flo, Janice, and Jeanine agreed.

"All agreed. Luther, we want you to be in charge of providing security for the preach-off."

"Alright, Charley. Agreed. One more thing. I'm going to need blueprints of the church building. I need to know all the rooms and entrances and exits. This will help as I school my troops."

Ted popped up. "I can get you those, Luther. You need anything else?"

"Thanks, Ted. That's it for now."

"If there's not anything else, I move we adjourn this meeting."

As they moved to leave, Jeanine approached Ted. "You want to go get some coffee?"

"Not tonight, Jeanine. I need to talk with Luther a little."

Jeanine was visibly crushed. After all she spent all afternoon in the beauty parlor and wore her best dress for this meeting. And all for naught!

Janice saw what was going on. "I'll go with you, Jeanine. Come on. That's such a pretty dress!"

The Blueprint

Ted did want to have a few words with Luther, but he used that as an excuse to get away from Jeanine. Like most men, Ted liked to do the chasing, not be the chased. His instincts when feeling pursued were to run or turn and fight. Right now, running seemed the safer and more gentle of his two choices. He saw Jeanine sag when he declined her invitation to coffee and regarded that as further proof that she was after him, her intentions thwarted.

He sighed, remembering something that Luther had told him about the martial arts. If you want someone to come close, give them plenty of room. Of all the women he knew, Flo and Viola seemed to understand that. Jeanine and Janice were another matter.

Oh well, he thought, on to other matters! Luther wanted a blueprint of the church building. Ted hadn't seen one for some years, but he thought one might be in the church attic. The attic was their place of storage since the basement was used for Sunday school classes, training union meetings, church suppers, Vacation Bible School, and other such events.

The next morning, after his breakfast of eggs, bacon, toast, and strong black coffee, Ted walked over to the church, enjoying a leisurely pace through the neighborhood with its sidewalks cracked from insistent tree roots, its front yards with flowers of many hues and varieties, the intoxicating aroma of honeysuckle, and the singing of birds greeting the early morning sun.

He almost hated to go inside, but Ted was a man who completed his mission. Once aimed somewhere, he followed through.

Ted pulled down the ladder to the attic and went up, his head poking through the opening, looking for the light switch he knew was there somewhere.

The attic was filled with boxes of old hymnals, church records, some broken chairs that were going to be mended someday, and several storage cabinets. It looked as if no one had been there for quite some time.

True to her word, Mrs. Felton, who had been the church secretary since Moses was barred from the promised land, had left her ring of keys in the middle drawer of her desk.

Ted fumbled with the keys until one fit and opened a storage cabinet. He saw the tightly coiled blueprints right away. He moved to an old table that had seen better days and unrolled the prints to make sure he had what he was looking for, an accurate depiction of the church layout. He gasped at what he found.

Hurriedly re-rolling his find, he closed and locked the cabinet and left the attic, hardly pausing to turn off the lights and push the ladder back up to its resting place. Ted was not an easily excitable man, but his heart was beating more quickly and his mind was racing. The documents under his arm were going to get a lot of folk stirred up! He needed to go see Charley right away!

If That Don't Beat All!

"Hi Ted! I came over as quickly as I could."

Ted had settled down a little, having gotten over the initial excitement of the discovery and its meaning. He had had some time to reflect since his phone call to Charley.

"Hi, Charley. Would you like a cup of coffee? I've got some fresh brewed."

Charley sat down at the kitchen table. "Sure. Make mine black. You sure sounded excited about something. Does this have any thing to do with the goofy way Jeanine was acting last night?"

Ted sighed, "I wouldn't exactly call my reaction to Jeanine 'exciting'. I'm *afraid* is more like it. No, I found something unexpected this morning when I went to get that blueprint for Luther."

"Was it something in the church attic? That place hasn't been cleaned up in years."

"That's what I thought too. When I asked Mrs. Felton for the keys to those cabinets up there, she said Bagston had been up there a lot before he died."

"Why would Bagston want to crawl around in that old attic? He usually left things like that to the janitor."

"It turns out he was hiding something up there. And probably going up to study over it from time to time. I not only found the blueprints I was looking for, but also a new set drawn up in the past year."

Charley snorted. "Lord, what else was Bagston up to? We seem to just keep uncovering his sins on a daily basis."

"His shenanigans seem to never end, don't they? He was up to something pretty major league. I have the new blueprints here. Take a look. They show plans for a huge shopping center with all the large chains represented plus an auto mall and a theme park."

"What? In this town? How in the world did Bagston expect to finance such an adventure?"

"He was selling out the church! If you look at the coordinates on the plans, the mall is designed to be built smack dab on top of the church and all its acreage. He was playing both ends against the middle. Promising the property to the mob and trying to make money for himself with a mall!"

"That old shyster! I suppose he stood to make himself some serious money off of this."

"Yes, and no doubt pay off some gambling debts. I suppose he thought he could make this happen through his charm and charisma. Just keep hammering away at the congregation and saying it was God's will. No doubt picking out Bible verses that would prove his point. But we will never know how he thought he would get away with this."

"Like leading the sheep to slaughter. I just can't believe how we were all so taken by him. Guess that's what happens when we take our eyes off of God and put them on a man."

"Or a woman." Ted was thinking of Jeanine and actually shuddering.

Charley chuckled. "That depends on which woman you have your eyes on."

Ted shook his head. "I know you are all taken up with Millie. But believe me, Charley, if you and Millie head in the direction I think you might be, you are going to wake up one morning and see her drooling on the pillow and wonder what in the world you got yourself into."

Charley was horrified. "I just can't see Millie like that. She's different."

"That's what they all say, Charley. Never mind me, I'm just an old curmudgeon. I've learned my lessons in that area, but you are a fresh young pup and I pray that your experiences will be different from mine."

Charley thought to himself, *Boy, some woman must have done a stomp on Ted's heart!* "Thanks, Ted. But let's get back to the blueprints. How much do you think Mayhew had his hands into this?"

"Good question! And one we need to have answered. We need to know how far along this has gone, who the other players are, and if anything has been signed."

" How do we find out?"

"A next step would be to contact the architectural firm that drew up these plans. Their name is right here in the corner. Looks like they are based in Atlanta. They can tell us who was involved in the meetings that led to the blueprints."

"Good idea, Ted. But don't we have to be careful what questions we ask? We don't want the wrong people to know we're snooping around."

"Too late for that. We are in the thick of it now. We just have to know who else is in the thicket."

"No telling where this will lead. Bagston was involved with some shady characters. And another thing. Do we tell anyone else about this? Or just keep it to ourselves?"

"I think after we get our facts together we should call an open church meeting and present what we know. Before we do that, we should have a meeting of the current credentials committee plus Viola and anyone else the committee wants to include."

"And one more thing, Charley. I also found a recent title search on the church property. I reckon whoever Bagston's partners were needed to make sure there are no prior claims on the property."

"This just gets bigger and bigger. You think we ought to present this to the church before the preach-off? I think that would scare off most folks. Looks like we need to raise all the money we can."

"Not so fast, Charley. I got some more to tell you. Something that we just might be able to use to put a fly in some speculator's ointment. The church is built on a Creek burial ground."

"On a what? How can that be?"

"That's what the title search shows. After I got back to the house this morning and called you, I did a Google search. Governor George Troup took over all the Creek lands back in 1825 in the Treaty of Indian Springs. Seems that a half-breed first cousin of Troup, William McIntosh, who was the son of a Scottish trader and a Creek woman, gave the land over."

"What does all that mean to us? Can that tribe reclaim the land? And who would the tribe be now anyway?"

"The good governor saw to it that no Creek were left to dispute anything. They were either killed outright or force marched west. All property is theft, Charley. All the land we 'own' was stolen, taken by force. Something else interesting happened during that time that might explain some of Bagston's bizarre behavior."

"What else? My head is swimming. You'd better pour me another cup of that strong coffee."

"I know how you feel. All this hit me like a lightning bolt. You want a little whiskey in there too?"

"No thanks! The last thing our church needs is another hypocritical preacher. Although, it sure is a temptation."

Ted laughs. "I guess I just wasn't thinking. Well, here's the final piece to it. At least all I know right now. The story has it that when all this happened with Troup and McIntosh, a Creek shaman asked for protection of the spirits for all Creek burial grounds. He especially asked that all of evil intent who ventured on such grounds be driven mad."

"Do you think that's what happened to Bagston?"

"I sure do."

"That explains a lot. How about some of the others around here? Do you think they've been affected too?"

"We all have a lot to repent of. Living on someone else's land who our ancestors murdered is one of them. So I think we have all been affected. It's the deeply selfish and unrepentant of anything at all who are most strongly affected."

"That makes sense. The founders of this church must have had some sort of dedication of the ground before building. You would have thought that prayers would have been said over it. I'm sure they did not know at the time that the land was taken from others."

"Oh, they knew. They just didn't think about it too much. The information I just gave you is public knowledge. Folk just get caught up in their own lives and tend to pay such things no heed."

"Well, what can we do about it now? How will all this affect our church?"

"I just don't know, Charley. I think a next step might be for you to consider calling a meeting of the credentials committee, since the church has entrusted them with a lot of responsibility. Plus whoever else you might think would be worth an invite at this point. I certainly recommend we include Viola."

"I'd hate to get *some* of our church members in on this. For now, let's just keep it confined to our committee. The less we tell, the better. I agree that Viola should be included. Will this change our preach-off plans? Can we just keep on with it?"

"That's what we need to discuss. It's not up to just you and me. I'm not so sure that the less we tell, the better. Full disclosure has its merits. But that's something we can all discuss."

"Well, we do have a few weeks before the preach-off is scheduled. Some plans have been made that can't be changed. We have already invited some pretty well-known preachers here, and we got in touch with CNN. They're already planning to be here."

"I know. That's why it is important to have a meeting as soon as possible, or am I misunderstanding? Do you wish to suppress this information until after the preach-off?"

"I just don't know, Ted. Both things are mighty important to the survival of our church. I guess we'll have a meeting as soon as we can get everybody together and let them decide. If we kept it under wraps, we'd be as guilty as McIntosh and Troup were."

"Yep. I agree. I am very pleased to have you as a friend, Charley. It helps tremendously to talk things out with someone you know and trust."

"I appreciate that. I've always valued you as a friend. Hey, you know what? I've just had a crazy idea. Maybe we could find some relatives of that Creek nation and invite them here for the preach-off. What do you think?"

"Yes!"

"I'm going to need your help with that, Ted. You seem to be a better researcher than me. Of course, I'll help you with anything I can. In fact, if the committee agrees with it, we can get them all involved."

"I think that it would be good if there is a Native American preacher at the preach-off too, maybe one of the Creek folk."

"Man, Ted! The Bible says that 'all things work together for good for them that love Him'. This was some pretty sorry mess before. Now I'm beginning to feel pretty good about it. Who knows what will come of this!"

Henry Wide Bear

Henry Wide Bear understood the foibles of humankind. Even as a boy, he had been keenly aware of the spiritual energies that made up each person – **all** the energies, daimonic and demonic. Henry easily saw through appearances into a person's inner core. His penetrating gaze caused some to squirm with discomfort at being seen, at having their souls laid bare. As a result, he had learned the value and the power of "soft eyes," a shaman-warrior way of seeing. Henry saw plenty enough with his peripheral vision.

When he first caught a glimpse of Viola Trumpett, he smiled. He saw a golden core opening outward into silver and blue with lightning flashes of red and black when she became agitated. He knew he was in the presence of another shaman.

Henry met Viola at a Wellness and Spirituality Conference in Tucson and liked her instantly. The conference, though focused on the well-being of Native Americans, was open to people of all cultures and backgrounds, both as presenters and as participants. Henry, like most folk, had not heard of spiritual criminology before, so found himself in Viola's workshop of that name.

An instant and enduring friendship sprang into being.

As a Creek shaman, Henry was not only connected with the Poarch Creek community in Alabama, but roamed freely throughout the northern and southern hemispheres of the Americas, visiting all tribes, all peoples. Henry considered that all humans belonged to the Navel Tribe, since all had that peculiar marking at their middle. "We are all plucked from the same vine and we have the scars to prove it," he would say laughingly.

As he rode into the little town with a family of Ojibwa who were coming down from the Upper Peninsula to visit some relations in Florida, Henry opened his heart to discerning Viola's intent in asking him here. When she appeared in the dream, she had only said she needed his help.

Henry and Viola

"Henry."

"Viola."

"Thanks for coming."

"You bet."

"Coffee?"

"That'd sure be good."

"Come on back to the kitchen."

The kitchen table and chairs were tubular chrome, the table top off-red and the padding for the chair seats and backs of the same color, as if Viola had gotten a deal at a closing out sale of a café from the 1950's.

The coffee was hot, strong, and black. Just like Henry liked it.

"We've got a situation here, Henry."

Henry understood immediately. Trouble. And with Viola involved, trouble in more than one dimension, certainly beyond the surface realm that most folk called reality.

Henry sipped his coffee.

"A man has died. Possibly murdered. Some evidence points to that. A number of people were not unhappy to see him go."

"I saw the news up there in Sault Sainte Marie. You guys are famous."

"We need your help, Henry. I'm hoping you will do a sweat for us."

"How many folk?"

"Maybe nine or ten. And none of them have ever done a sweat before."

They sat quietly for a while listening to the singing of the cicadas through the back door screen.

"Let's take a look at your back yard."

"Okay. And Henry?"

Henry paused at the door.

"One of them may be a murderer."

Phil Rock Boy

Phil Rock Boy gave Henry a hand in selecting and collecting the sapling river willows that would be used in constructing the sweat lodge frame. Phil, a Lakota Sioux, had served in the Marines as a forward observer for naval gunfire. He loved to hear the large shells splitting the air overhead and the anticipation of their explosive release as they hit their designated targets. Others carried .45s and M-1s as their weapons. Phil carried a warship.

Like most warriors, Phil was a peaceful man. After his discharge from the Marines, Phil used his saved up funds to buy a few acres with a cabin in the forest not too far from the river. He and Luther Huckleberry were friends but most of the folk in the little Anglo community neither knew of nor cared about his existence. Among his Lakota kin in North and South Dakota, he was known both for his good humor and his stubborn nature.

The two men rode in Phil's old pickup, his "pride and joy" he called it, to town and pulled into Viola's driveway. Their presence did not go unnoticed amongst Viola's neighbors, who had already been treated to an unloading of seasoned logs and select rocks Phil had on hand from previous sweats he had conducted at his place. Sweats no Anglos had attended.

A fire pit had been dug in Viola's large back yard, after carefully removing the sod for later replacement. The logs were burning merrily, heating the rocks for that evening's ceremony. Viola was in attendance and already had a large pitcher of iced tea for them on the nearby picnic table in the shade of a large chinaberry tree.

The two men worked quietly and with practiced skill rooting the strong, flexible saplings into a circular formation around the hole that would hold the hot rocks during the sweat. The saplings were bent over and tied to create a dome frame. Tarps and blankets were laid over the frame creating a snug and dark spiritual space.

Viola had been making the tobacco ties and they were put in place. Phil had previously brought over the bucket and dipper and a deer antler that Henry would use plus a pitch fork for Phil to transport the hot rocks into the lodge.

"I think we are ready, Viola." said Henry.

Sweat Invites

Now that the sweat lodge had been properly set up in her backyard, Viola knew the greater task of inviting people to the sweat lay ahead of her. She had to go about this carefully. Most people in the South had never heard of such a thing. Although, the building of the lodge had caused quite a stir. Viola wanted those who could be guilty of murdering Bagston there. How could she be sure all would be there without arousing their suspicions that one of them was about to be exposed? At least that was the hope. She would not give them too much information about the sweat. Maybe their curiosity would get them to come.

So far she knew that Henry Wide Bear, Phil Rock Boy and herself would attend.

Of course, Luther wouldn't miss it. He had always wanted to be a part of making some of these folks sweat anyway. He had done his best in the past.

Viola contacted Thelma first. Not because Thelma was a prime suspect, but because her history with voodoo would make it almost impossible for her to refuse. She would have been afraid not to. After all, Viola had that chicken leg around somewhere.

Thelma went home and asked Junior about coming to the sweat. Junior wanted no part of it. Though his and Thelma's relationship had become based more on love and respect, Junior still said no to this request. "Heck, Thelma, if I wanted to sweat, I'd go weed the vegetable garden like you've been wanting me to. I think you gotta be half out of your mind to want to go sit in a teepee with them heathens just so you can be hot! I ain't going!"

"Well, would you mind if I went?" Thelma was working hard on being mindful of Junior's feelings.

"No, go on ahead. If it makes you happy, it's alright with me. But if those heathens bother you in any way, they'll have me to answer to!" Thelma was pleased that Junior was now acting as her protector.

Flo, Janice, Charley, Millie, and Ted were the next to receive invitations, each one gratefully accepting and very much looking forward to the experience. Viola knew there was no use in asking Evelyn to come. She had never been considered a suspect. And Evelyn would not even consider getting sweaty with men present. Besides it would ruin her new perm.

Mayhew's Mayhem

Excitement was building to a fever pitch in this small town. And it wasn't just the Baptists that were working so hard. Folk from every denomination were getting in on the doings.

The ladies in the Women's Club were baking cakes, cookies and making gallons of iced tea and lemonade for the visitors that would be coming to the preach-off. Of course, a small donation was expected for these refreshments.

The Junior League along with the town council had started a clean up campaign. They decided to call it "Clean up, clean up for Jesus". That way, any objectors would be seen as heathens.

Local merchants were asked to have their stores shining brightly for the coming affair. Windows were rubbed clean. Why they even washed down the buildings! Not a speck of trash in sight.

Spitting on the sidewalks was absolutely forbidden during this time and a stiff fine would be given to anyone who tried. Chewing tobacco or dipping snuff was a thing to be done at home or on your own front porch. The usual game of checkers played outside the courthouse was banned, because those old men couldn't play checkers without a good size chaw in their cheeks.

This town wanted to display a clean shining image to the world who would be watching them so closely. Kinda like those who put on their godly face to the world and acted like the devil at home.

Everyone was caught up in the excitement. Their focus was on cleaning the town and the providing for visitors who were to come. Seems each one had their own idea of how to make a buck or two from this coming preach-off. They were bound to see that someone besides the church was going to make a profit.

Luther and his security gang also had their focus on their job at hand. And it was a good thing they did.

The town was already teeming with visitors. Miss Clara's boarding house was full as was the motel on Highway 29. The news media had brought their trailers to camp in for the duration. The cash registers in town were continuously ringing as their drawers were stuffed with more money than the local merchants had ever seen.

The day before the first scheduled preacher a good number of the townspeople were at the church finishing up final preparations. The choir was practicing. Some of the women were arranging tables in the fellowship hall for the sale of refreshments, and some were putting the last coat of furniture polish on the church pews and communion table. Yes sir, this thing was going to work. Their church and their town would be saved from the imposing evil. Or so they thought.

Just as Ethel was about to hit her high note in the song the choir was practicing for tomorrow's service, a loud explosion was heard and smoke began to rise from the basement. It shook the whole foundation of the church. The women screamed and some of the men let out words that before they had reserved for their usual discussions about politics or football.

Before anyone could react to the calamity, Luther and his guys were already in control. They had been patrolling the area in anticipation of just such a problem. Luther had caught Freddy coming out of the basement and had him in a choke hold. Freddy's eyes were bulging out. If he could have gotten his breath, he would have begged for mercy or tried to con Luther into thinking he had been near the church for some benevolent reason.

"Don't you even open your mouth, slime ball." Luther was hoping Freddy would try to make a move against him.

"You thought you could come in here and shut this thing down, didn't you? Well, Freddy boy, you ain't fooling with one of them turn-the-other-cheek pushovers."

Several men sent by Mayhew were also caught sneaking around. The security team had them sprawled on the lawn and hogtied.

The local fire department rushed to the scene and entered the basement to evaluate the damage. Fortunately, Freddy was no demolition expert and the charge he set off was not enough to do anything but blow out a window and fill the basement with smoke. He was so inept at his task that he had used a short fuse and didn't get out of the basement before the blast singed his eyebrows right off.

"Luther, what in the world happened?" Charley had been in the sanctuary and was one of the first to come around the building, when he saw grown men trussed up like hogs for the killing and Freddy all red and minus his facial hair.

"Nothing to worry about Charley. I told you things were going to get rough."

"Anybody hurt?" Charley asked.

"Naw. Just this joker. He won't have to worry about clipping his nose hairs for quite a while." Luther had not released his hold and Freddy was turning redder by the minute.

"Not much damage here, Charley." The fire chief had come out of the basement after his inspection. "You lost one window, but no fire damage."

"Well, thank God for that!" Charley heaved a sigh of relief.

"God ain't the only one you have to thank, Charley. If me and the boys hadn't been here, it could have been worse. The sheriff is on his way to take them to jail."

Just then all two of the town's sheriff cars pulled up at the curb.

"Mayhew should hear about this when ol' Freddy here makes his call to a lawyer at the station, Charley. You can be sure it will be one of Mayhew's shysters. I don't think he'll have the nerve to try anything else now. I'm sure Bubba over at the sheriff's office will have these guys singing like birds."

Preach-Off: Gregor's Sermon

In his deep inner being, Gregor knew that he had doomed himself into his current condition, a remarkable insight for a demon. He had been, even more than now, a rebellion hellion. But Gregor carried a small glimmer of light, a teeny sliver of hope, even though hope and light caused his dark heart burning pain.

Oh, it was still easy for him to lapse into blame of others for his devilish predicament. He had full access to and continued to wallow in the seven deadly sins of Christianity, to cultivate the unwholesome mental factors and cognitive afflictions warned against in Buddhism, to delight in the infidel status ascribed to him by the Quran, and to enjoy being the poster demon child warned against by all religions and spiritual paths.

But Gregor knew that the Universe has an excellent recycling program. These bursts of insight came from a unique event – the visit of Jesus to Hell. Gregor had been present when the visit occurred and his future had changed forever.

In the church bulletin all had received from the diligent ushers at the little church's front door, they saw that Gregor's sermon was entitled "Rescued From Hell."

After the required prayers and announcements and hymn singing and the taking of the offering, Gregor took the pulpit. His deep bass voice rolled through the congregation.

"Have you ever been in that place where life itself is like a living hell? I'll bet everyone here has felt that at one time or another. (Nods of agreement) Well, I've been in that place a lot. In fact at one time I was a prisoner there.

(He had their attention right away with that remark.)

But I wouldn't be talking with you here today if that was all there was to it. You know how they say that in the darkest night a candle glows? (Amens were spoken.) And every cloud has a silver lining?

I'm here to tell you that there is a little bit of heaven in the depths of hell! (Not a single amen on that one. It went against popular theology. But Ted began to smile.)

Now you might not be used to thinking that way. I hope I can make it clearer to you here tonight.

My life was once in the pits! But something happened and I stand before you now. I think you will be startled by my story.

Will you please turn in your Bibles to Isaiah 24:22?

It says, "*And they shall be gathered together, as prisoners are gathered in the pit, and shall be shut up in the prison, and after many days shall they be visited.*"

That's the pit I'm talking about! Imagine yourself down in that pit milling around in the foul waste of yourself and others, sleep-deprived, taken out and tortured, agonizing over your unknown fate.

(Junior nudged Thelma, "Is he one of those Ay-rabs we captured?" "Hush, Junior! Just listen!")

And then, wonder of wonders, totally unexpected, you get a visitor!

I don't know if you grasp the full implications of that. You are alone, without hope, the only thing keeping you going is some kind of stubbornness deep inside that won't give up. Days and nights go by indistinguishable from each other. All you know is suffering and uncertainty and fear.

Then you notice a difference in the atmosphere. The pit-keepers seem both agitated and excited. You are taken with the others and hosed down with cold water, washing away your filth. Clean prison garb is given.

The word is in the air. Visitor! A visitor is coming! All of a sudden you are reminded that there are worlds other than the hell you are in. Your head lifts up a little bit. Something begins to stir in the numbness – the numbness that has allowed you to survive.

It's like when your arm has gone to sleep from laying on it the wrong way and that feeling like tingling painful needles that shoot through when it begins to wake up.

Except that now it's not your arm, it's your soul. The familiar numbness can seem more like your friend than this painful awakening.

(The congregation gave him full attention now. They knew exactly what he was talking about.)

The Visitor was unlike anyone I have ever met. He was powerful, of radiant heart and mind. His eyes were piercing but emanated a force, an energy I knew little about. His gaze would have been unbearable except for his deliberate softening of its intensity. For the first time in my life, I knew mercy. I knew love.

(Eyes were tearing up. Tissues were retrieved from purses, handkerchiefs from pockets.)

It didn't take me long to understand the purpose of His visit. You can read it for yourself in Isaiah 42:7.

(Gregor allowed folk time to find it. Many of them being good Baptists and having participated in Sword Drills in the Sunday evening Training Union found the passage immediately.)

I will read it aloud. *"To open the blind eyes, to bring out the prisoners from the prison, and them that sit in darkness out of the prison house."*

(People began murmuring. Who was this preacher? That verse they just read was generally interpreted as referring to Jesus. Was he saying he was there when Jesus visited hell?)

Some in our group stayed in their numbness, not ready to hear what he had to say. Others, like me, attuned to him right away.

I know what you are thinking. Is this true? Did Jesus really preach to those in hell?

First Peter 3:18 through 20 says that after Jesus' crucifixion he was *"quickened by the Spirit: By which also he went and preached unto the spirits in prison; Which sometime were disobedient."*

Jesus had just gone through hell on earth. Tortured in the worst way possible. Abandoned by everyone. By everyone! So he knew what hell was. And when he came to visit, we knew he knew. That made all the difference. In a sense he was one of us.

(People were spellbound now, not knowing what to think. You could almost hear the sparking fizzle of minds short-circuiting.)

Now I know you are going to be judging me, once all this sinks in. Not only is it the nature of humans to pass judgment, though Jesus taught not to do so, but in this case, my case, it is foretold in the scripture I am about to read.

My last Bible text for this preach-off sermon (Gregor was reminding people where they were, bringing them out of the hell-visitation imagery to the here and now) is I Peter 4:6. *"For this cause was the gospel preached also to them that are dead, that they might be judged according to men in the flesh, but live according to God in the spirit."*

Jesus visited hell to preach the gospel, the "good news." And some of us heard it and some of us didn't. Those of us who heard stayed behind and talked with him a little more.

He told us many things. I share two with you. He said that we had done so much wrong that we would always be judged harshly by most people. We understood that and accepted it. But he also said that we were not to be taken down by those judgments.

And this is the really good news! We did not have to stay in hell but could "live according to God in the spirit!"

And if that is true for demons in hell, think how true it is for you!

Brother Ted, will you lead us in prayer?

"Heavenly Father, we are thankful for this message we have heard preached here tonight. We ask your blessings on the one who delivered it. Everyone of us here has been in one hell or another in our brief lives here on earth. And we greatly appreciate your mercy and lovingkindness in visiting us there. We know that we are the ones who give ourselves hell, not you. All we get from you is life and breath and forgiveness and joy. Thank you for you, Dear God. Amen!"

Ted's Sermon

They had come, like all good Baptists everywhere, for their souls to be both fed and entertained. These folk were connoisseurs of the sermon, appreciators of the spoken magic that turns metaphysical mysteries into simple understanding and routine daily actions into acts of God. Having heard tens of thousands of sermons in their church-filled lives, they were more than empty vessels waiting to be filled. They could tune out, go to sleep while generally maintaining facial expressions of benign interest and wakeful presence, drift into other realms unless the preacher kept it interesting and alive. A tough and discerning audience.

So he began.

"*When I was a child I spoke as a child, understood as a child, thought as a child, but when I became a man I put away childish things.*" Very few of us still carry around our blankie or teddy bear or a sugar teat or still suck our thumbs. Very few of us walk around with a pocket full of marbles or jacks. Very few of us still pull out our stacks of comic books to read and trade. As we get older we put those things away.

I'm going to make you mad this evening. I'm going to point out a childish thing you have not put away. You are going to get mad and you are going to get alarmed. You are going to be like children whose favorite toy is taken away. Some of you will hear. Some will understand.

Here it is in a nutshell. God assumed human form on earth to redeem **himself.**

Now most of you think and most of you have been taught that God took on human form, incarnated, to redeem **you.** If you reflect on that for a moment, that is rather self-centered. It's all about you. God took human form to save YOU.

This way of thinking is not only self-centered but it goes even further in its absurdity. Save you from what? Why to save you from God's wrath! This is a little peculiar, folk! God set himself up to be killed so as to save you from his anger?

Now the standard party line is that we deserved his anger. Folks, that is the way it always is in an abusive relationship. The one abused feels like they deserve to be abused! They trot out their list of characteristics of which they feel ashamed and make the case against themselves that they deserve even worse than they've been getting. They even see the abuse as a sign of love. No one has paid so much attention to them before.

Let's take a look at God's own progress in his relationship with us and why he felt the need to redeem himself. Please turn in your Bibles to the book of Job. Yes! I said "God's own progress." I know there is a doctrine out there that God doesn't change. But I'm telling you, my friends, that God IS change. Always unfolding. Always emerging. He is the Wellspring of all existing. As a wellspring, as the Wellspring, he is always springing.

In the book of Job, we see God as an abuser. He listens to the voice of Satan. He breaks his own commandments. He becomes a party to robbery, to murder, to willful abuse of the innocent. And then turns a deaf ear to Job's pleas for justice. (Notice! Job did not ask for mercy. He only wanted justice!)

Job had nowhere to turn. He was being tortured beyond belief with the full approval of God. All he could do was ask God to make a case against Himself.

God's response? He became even more bullying! He came roaring in asking who did Job think he was to question him? Just an insignificant little worm! All Job could do was submit. His abuser was too powerful.

Job claimed the moral high ground over God on that one.

God created this pesky little critter, the human. And what makes us so pesky? Free will! Freedom of choice. So we get into the most peculiar situations, situations that God would never have gotten into by himself.

Now here's you a thought you might not have thunk before. God learns from us. The way we are creates a difference in him.

Oh no! you might be thinking. God is omniscient, all wise. He can't learn anything more. He already knows everything.

Think about it, folks. Already knowing everything can be the most boring thing there is! Nothing new to discover. No freshness of spirit. Sitting in the cosmic classroom at a too small desk, your knees bumping your chin, while the teacher asks you to recite the alphabet one more time. Your eyes roll up into your head with boredom!

God is all wise all right, wise enough to be a great adventurer! Why even this universe of which we are a part is expanding outward meeting and entering relationship with the unknown! God has set it up this way, folks! A continuous meeting and greeting and learning.

So God learned from Job. He began to see this human had a point. This human had a perspective on things God didn't have. So God decided to become a human, to be born on earth in human form.

And why? Not to redeem humans, thought that would be a secondary effect, but to redeem himself. Now that's the kind of God I like! That's the God I love! And he truly understood what it is like to be one of us when he cried from the cross in great anguish, totally alone, just like Job -- "My God! My God! Why have you forsaken me?"

At that point, God redeemed himself with Job, redeemed himself from his old arrogant behavior, and became the God we now know and love, the God who would have mercy and not sacrifice.

Jesus' words in Matthew 12:7 spoken to the Pharisees could just as easily have been spoken to Yahweh in his dealings with Job: *"But if ye had known what this means, I will have mercy, and not sacrifice, ye would not have condemned the guiltless."*

Now this may be a fresh thought with you, because you have been all wise, your mind made up like a bed in the morning. You have created an image of God, against all advice, and plan to worship that image to the death (which it is).

God can change too, folks. God is more mysterious than any of us can think. God is ever changing, ever unfolding. And we are partners with him on this Great Adventure, this Grand Endeavor.

Let us pray.

Luther's Sermon

"I know some of y'all don't think I should be up here, but I'll just tell you some of Jesus' words, "No prophet is accepted in his own country" (that's Luke 4:24 for you Bible toters) and I'll add to that a more recent saying "An expert is somebody from some place other than here."

"Can anything good come out of Nazareth?" was the way they put it in Jesus' time. If you answer "No" you are taking the side of those same idiot mouth-breathing gossiping yoyos in Jesus' day. You know who I'm talking about and if you truly were a Christian you would come down to the altar and ask for forgiveness right now instead of waiting for some altar call.

I don't ask for forgiveness for saying these things because they are true.

Now that we have that elephant in the room identified, rather than just pretending it doesn't exist, let me go on to something more spiritually edifying.

The text for today is Luke 4:14 – 30.

When you take a look at that entire chapter, at the 29 verses leading up to Luke 4:30, you will find that Jesus had just come in from the wilderness where he had been eye-to-eye with the Devil and had stared him right down. The contest went three rounds and Jesus whipped him every round. No need for a technical decision by any referees either. Jesus floored him every time, and at the end of round three knocked him right out of the ring.

(Luther delivered that with such deep and sincere enthusiasm that Junior, being both a Jesus lover and a fight fan, jumped to his feet and yelled "Amen!" Others were feeling what Junior felt and were about to let go with some amens of approval, but Junior beat them to the punch with such vigor he spoke for them all.)

So Jesus returned to Galilee. It wadn't no ordinary just-kind-of-lazing-into-town return either! The Bible says that "Jesus returned in the power of the Spirit!" And that is spelled with a capital S, folks! And it doesn't say *a* Spirit. It says *the* Spirit! Jesus wadn't filled with the power of just any old spirit. He was filled with the power of THE Spirit!

(Resounding amen's from all over the sanctuary. Folk were into the message now, had forgotten for the moment who was even preaching.)

So here he comes to his home town, "where he had been brought up." Word of his coming had preceded him. He had just had a great evangelistic tour through the entire area, "*and there went out a fame of him through all the region round about. And he taught in their synagogues, being glorified of all.*"

The hometown folk in Nazareth had a lot of expectations. But they had some things backwards. Rather than being ready to glorify Jesus, they were eagerly awaiting Jesus to come and glorify them! And you know Jesus, he could see into people's hearts. He knew what they were feeling, what they were thinking.

I think too they had treated Jesus badly as a boy. Whispering that he was an illegitimate child, a bastard! (The older ladies began fanning their faces much more rapidly, unaccustomed to such a word being spoken from the pulpit.) So you know what they were calling his mother! The gossips all talked about how good Joseph, Jesus' step-daddy, was in keeping the family together in spite of Mary's bad behavior.

So Jesus didn't have it easy growing up in that town. He was ridiculed. His mama was talked bad about. And when his step-daddy died, Jesus, being the oldest child, took on the responsibility of taking care of the family.

On the Sabbath day, Jesus went to the synagogue there in downtown Nazareth and was asked to read the scripture. He was given the book of Isaiah. He opened it and read from Chapter 61. He read the first verse and only the first part of verse two.

The Spirit of the Lord is upon me; because he hath anointed me to preach the gospel to the poor; he hath sent me to heal the brokenhearted, to preach deliverance to the captives, and recovering of sight to the blind; to set at liberty them that are bruised, To proclaim the acceptable year of the Lord.

It was both an announcement and a teaser. After reading it aloud, Jesus did two things. The first thing he did was close the book, return it to the minister, and sit down. He didn't elaborate. He didn't tell them any more. He didn't walk around amongst them and start doing healing. He closed the book on them and sat down!

They all sat there looking at him.

The second thing he did was tell them this scripture is fulfilled **this day**. Which meant he was claiming it as pertaining to him. To this crowd though, he said this scripture is fulfilled "in your ears." Not in their hearts. In their ears! That's as far as it got. The message stopped at their ears.

You know the rest of the story. Jesus said, "You want these things done here. But it's not going to happen."

Now I don't think Jesus was bearing a grudge, though he did have his dark side. The reason things couldn't happen there that happened when Jesus was telling the good news in the other towns was people's hearts were closed.

That's made plain when you look at their reaction. Instead of saying, "Lord, help us! We've really messed up," they jumped up, grabbed him, took him out to the edge of town, and were going to throw him over a cliff!

Some folk don't like it when you tell them the truth.

But Jesus was the world's first Aikido master. *"Passing through the midst of them he went his way."* They couldn't touch him.

My main point is this, folks. There are good-hearted loving people in this town who, because they are not of high social status, are talked bad about and slighted when you pass them on the street. If Jesus were in the flesh here, he would be hanging out with them and not the slighters and slack-jawed gossipers.

Remember that Jesus went to those "outside the camp." His buddies were ruffians and street people and prostitutes and tax collectors. Yes, he was friends with some well-to-do folk, but his first love was for people who were just what they were, nothing more. And for some reason, these are usually the folk of low social standing.

Why the reason you are having this preach-off is because you got scammed by somebody at the top of the social totem pole!

My invitation to you is to stop listening with your ears and start listening with your hearts. That way Jesus won't go sit down and tell you what you are looking for just ain't going to happen. When you open your hearts to each other, you can see the truth and you won't fall into the mess you've gotten yourself into now! I'll do my best to do the same.

What's happened in this town can be a blessing to all of us.

Thank you for letting me speak here in this preach-off.

Janice's Sermon

Charley knew that the credentials committee had decided that women would be able to speak at the preach-off. He had no problem with that. At least he didn't until Janice Bagston came to him and asked for her name to be put on the list to deliver a sermon.

Introducing Janice to the congregation as the speaker of the night was not something that he looked forward to doing. She certainly needed no introduction, and it was not her first time to let her feelings be known before the whole church. Charley shuddered as he remembered the church conference. He was not sure how the congregation would react when he called her name to deliver a message. Would they laugh at him as if he had played a colossal joke on them? Or would they boo her off the stage? Whatever, he was the pastor and it was his job.

When the time came, Charley had already decided to make his introduction brief. The only reactions to it were a few dropped jaws and a couple of forced coughs. Janice made her way to the podium in a sedate, ladylike manner. Her voice was soft as she began, "My sermon to you is more of an apology. If you listen, I believe you will hear in it truth and a sermon that only the example of one's life can preach.

I sat in a pew in this church for many years listening to my husband pretend to proclaim the word of God. All the while I knew what kind of man he was and how his personal life was anything but godly. You know now as well as I do what he was involved in. This whole church was hurt by him in so many ways. We almost lost this building because of him.

His crimes against you and against God were great. He did not believe what he preached. He was to be the protector of this flock, but he was the one doing the most harm. Your shepherd was keeping company with the wolves. I can't say he was living a double life, because he was only living one life… one of self-service and sin. He was never really your pastor and my husband. That was only pretense.

Bagston led you astray, but I sat by and kept my mouth shut. I let my concern for my own reputation stop me from exposing him for what he was. That's why I asked to speak to you today. Bagston was guilty of grievous spiritual crimes for which I believe he is paying right now. But, I too, am guilty of spiritual crimes. Maybe not the ones he committed, but ones just as harmful. I harmed myself and I harmed others.

You looked up to me because of my position as the pastor's wife. In fact, I insisted that you look up to me. Controlling folks became like a game to me. The rush I got from that game went to my head and I lost any perspective of the fact that I was using you to feed my own ego. To me, that is one of the worst spiritual crimes. Love for others is no where to be found in such actions. We are commanded in God's Word to love one another, to love our neighbors as ourselves. I did not do that. For that, I am grievously sorry.

After Bagston's death, there seemed to be nothing that I wouldn't do and with no care of what anyone thought. Still I misjudged and hurt people. If I called them all by name, we would be here all night. But I say to you all here in this assembly and before the whole world watching by television, that I have seen the harm I have done to you and to myself. I have realized now that we are all human beings, whether we are Christians or not. And no one has the right to judge another. We all struggle in this life, and I have come to know that we should take those struggles to God. I cannot use the problems of other people to inflate my own ego or to amuse myself. Seeing my brothers and sisters in trouble should inspire me to help them not slander them. I have asked God's forgiveness and I now ask yours.

We are about to begin again here in this church with a new pastor and a clear title. We want to be free from our unpleasant past. We will want others to join in our worship here and to know our God and what He can do in their lives. How can we expect them to come if they are going to be judged? If we are to be representatives of God, we must show His love. Now, you know me well enough to know that I am not talking about syrupy, superficial love. I'm talking about God's love that only He can put in us. Then, people will want to come. And then this church will be fulfilling its true purpose. We are the church, not this building. Lives are precious to God and they should be to us too."

Little Jimmie's Sermon

The last day of the preach-off was finally here. Little Jimmie Gallup from the Church of the Everlasting Seeking was one of the first preachers to sign up. However, he did demand to be the speaker on the last day. Little Jimmie thought that would give him the most publicity. CNN had already caught wind of the plight of the little Southern church. Jimmie was sure he would be the preacher with the largest crowd and would raise the most money. In his mind, no one else could top him.

He arrived with his full entourage. It was quite a show. Most folks had never seen so much commotion over one person. Those who hoped to have a private word with him couldn't even get close. His hairdresser, manicurist, script writer, and most important, his financial advisor got his full attention. He also had his own cook and nutritionist with him. Jimmie had to keep up his trim figure so he could fit into those hideous white suits he wore.

As you would suspect, his entrance into the pulpit was planned to be a flawless spectacle. He stepped out of his trailer and an assistant cued the release of a flock of white doves. A choir of 50 wearing golden robes followed him into the church singing 'Shall We Gather at the River' while the orchestra played so loudly that some thought surely the Lord was on His way to get them.

Jimmie had the whole congregation on their feet and clapping as if some rock star had arrived. Well, not all the congregation. A few of them just stood and looked as they sized up the gaudy show. Millie, Flo, Viola, Charley and Ted were in the skeptical number.

The choir followed Jimmie to the pulpit and surrounded him with arms outstretched. They looked like a choir of angels who focused only on Little Jimmie. As they got quiet, a trumpet was cued to blow and Little Jimmie stepped up to the microphone. "Brothers and Sisters, I have come here today to save you from despair and degradation! This day will live on in your memories and you will share it with your children and grandchildren. I am here! All your problems are solved!" The choir sang a rousing "Amen" and the trumpet blew again.

"My children! I know you find it hard to seat yourselves in the presence of such awesomeness, but I ask that you try." Once again, Jimmie had gotten carried away with himself. His voice had taken on a sanctimonious cadence. "I hope you are ready for the word I have for you today. This message came to me as I walked the floor on many sleepless nights. It is one of my finest sermons. Consider yourselves blessed!"

Millie's Interruption

Little Jimmie Gallup went into one of his dances that he was famous for. He gave the crowd his best show. The golden-robed choir clapped in time to the orchestra as Jimmie jumped, turned, twisted, and leaped, all to the delight of the audience. Miss Evelyn began to shout and raise her hands, wanting people to see that she was feeling the spirit. She found this even better for an attention getter than her regular visit to the altar.

"Stop!" A voice was heard in a small corner of the church. Most were so caught up in the show that they paid no attention. "Stop!!" The voice rang out even louder now. Some people got quiet, others just kept on clapping and chanting.

It was Millie Huckleberry who was shouting. She was making her way to the podium with a more than determined look on her face. As she approached Little Jimmie, she grabbed him by the shoulders and again shouted, "Stop!" There was an immediate hush over the congregation, except for the gasps of disbelief. What was Millie thinking by touching such a holy man while in the middle of his spirit-filled dance? It even took Little Jimmie a minute or two to realize what just happened. This was the first time anyone had ever wanted to stop him. And he was giving his best performance ever.

"Why, what do you mean, young lady? Just who do you think you are? Do you know *who* I am!?" Little Jimmie was just about to signal for some of his body guards to take Millie away, when Charley appeared beside Millie.

Charley said in a bold voice, "She knows who you are alright. I suggest you listen to her."

Little Jimmie wasn't one for confrontations. No one had dared challenge him before. Besides Charley bested him in physical size. So he nodded to his aides that everything was okay.

"Alright, Millie, go ahead and speak now. I don't believe anyone will stop you." Charley took his seat on the podium.

"Thank you, Charley." Millie realized that all eyes were on her. She had their full attention. The old Millie would have fled in tears. If she could have gotten out any words, they would have been weak and in the form of an apology. But the old Millie didn't exist anymore. Maybe she never did exist.

Little Jimmie and his band of golden angels slowly exited the stage. The congregation got quiet and sat down.

"What are we doing here? Just how important is money to us? Jesus got angry at the moneychangers in the temple making a profit for themselves off of worshippers. And He ran them out. How is this any different? We have been willing to desecrate the house of God for the sake of bringing in a few dollars. The whole world is watching us over television. Is this the image we want to give them of the God we worship? Is this circus side show an example of our evangelism to the world? Why would anyone want to serve a God like that?

Mind you, we have had some wonderful speakers here during this preach-off. Godly men. Men who spoke the Word of God with integrity. They put the spotlight on Almighty God and not themselves. And we have had some not-so-godly speakers. Yes, Gregor, I recognize you as the man who came to me that night in my dream! I know who you represent. Believe me, folks, this man definitely knows what he's talking about when he mentions hell!" People gasped as if they were actually choking on Millie's words. Gregor got up and moved quickly for the door. No one dared to stop him.

Millie continued, "My brother, Luther, brought a good message, though some of you didn't want to hear what he has to say because he is not a regular church goer. He talked about people who are not so socially accepted. We are all guilty of holding some people up in too high regard while so many people have suffered at the attitudes of so-called Christians who are just Pharisees. That religious group was the ones who wanted to put Jesus on trial and kill Him.

We have all been so concerned about the death of Bro. Bagston. Some think he was murdered. I agree with this theory. But the greatest crime committed here is that of trying to set ourselves up as our own god and expecting people to bow down to us. Little Jimmie was showing an example of how we act in our daily lives. We prance around like peacocks. Then when people try to touch us, we come back with the same attitude… "Who do you think you are? Do you know who I am?" Why can't we treat others with love and mercy, just like Jesus has for us?

God did not send His only Son into this world so that we could be like rock stars. He said in Matthew 5:16, "*Let your light so shine before men, that they may see your good works, and glorify your Father which is in heaven.*" What glory are we bringing to God when we hurt others and manipulate them? What glory do we bring to Him when we give the honor and worship to humans that belongs to Him?

The greatest crime we commit is that of wounding others and setting some up as objects of worship. The Bible tell us in Romans 3:23, "*For all have sinned, and come short of the glory of God.*" That means everyone!

I think it's time we searched our hearts, spent some time alone with God, and decided what our real purpose is here in this church. What good is all the money we raise if we are just going to build on the same old worldly foundation? If so, send the money back, close the doors, and let those mobsters build their casino here. Then you'll have a true form of human recreation that's full of winners and losers. Let's not let our church be that. Our foundation needs to be on that of Jesus Christ and none other.

That's all I have to say.

Sweat Lodge

Viola's living room and kitchen were crowded with nervous and excited folk. None had been in a sweat lodge before and didn't know what to expect -- of themselves or of the experience. Luther, Henry, and Phil were sitting quietly and calmly at the kitchen table.

Viola was met with many questions. What exactly do we do? Will we see ghosts? She assured them that everything would be okay and that Wide Bear would lead them in the adventure. "I hope everyone brought their bathing suits as requested," she said. "Some sweats are conducted in the nude, but that is for sweats of people of the same gender."

A sigh of relief came over this gathering of southerners of rather strict upbringings. Although, mixed bathing was looked down on too by older Baptists. This taboo went right along with dancing and hand holding in church.

"Any other questions?" asked Viola.

There were many questions but no one wanted to ask them. They decided to just wait and see how this went. All followed Henry outside. Phil was already taking on his responsibilities as fire tender, care giver for those in the sweat, and outside guard. He was removing the embers and remaining burning logs from the red-hot rocks with his pitchfork.

Jeanine thought "Fire and pitchfork! What kind of devilish thing have I gotten into!?"

Luther was having a heyday watching the expressions on the faces of the others. It was hard for him to hold in the laughter.

Henry asked everyone to stand in a circle outside the lodge. The moon was new and there were stars aplenty. They stood in silence for a while. Henry said, "I know this is new for you, but you are prayerful people of good souls and intent. You will be fine. In a few moments we will go inside."

"Enter to the left and move around the circle so that the first one entering will stop and take a seat just to the right of the opening." Henry gestured with his hands as to how they were to do this. His imitation of crawling helped break the ice.

"We will have silent prayer for a few moments and then go in. I will take a seat in the middle. Then Phil will give us a rock on the pitchfork. He knows what he is doing. Your job is to sit very still. I will rake the rock into the hole with this deer antler. I figure tonight we will use only five rocks. That will be plenty enough. Before we pray and then enter, do you have any questions?"

They were silent because they felt they were in good hands and all questions they had would be answered in due time.

They stood in silent prayer each searching her or his own heart then entered the lodge and sat quietly, while Phil and Henry positioned each rock in the hole at the center. The rocks were glowing red and all felt the intense heat instantly.

After the last rock, Phil closed the flap. Henry took a dipper of water and poured it gently on the rocks while singing a prayer in his own language. The lodge instantly filled with steam.

"Use the sage I gave you in the kitchen," he said. You can chew its leaves if you want. Or you can just hold it to your nose for its scent and its healing powers. If the heat begins to get too intense, put your towel in front of your face."

"In a while, I will call for Phil to open the flap and let some outside air in. If you need to have the flap opened, do you remember the Lakota phrase I told you that is the signal?"

"Mitakuye Oyasin!" said Jeanine who was sure she was about to call it out right now.

Henry began to sing and chant -- his voice rising to the heights then dropping into a strong clear bass. He poured another dipper of water on the rocks. The steam hissed and expanded throughout the lodge, entering and cleansing as it went. The rocks had lost their red color and the lodge was pitch black.

Flo began to get a little uneasy. The solemn atmosphere brought her mind to things in her life that she regretted. She had hated Bagston so fiercely. *Would anyone find out what her plans were for him?*

Janice wondered to herself what Bagston would think if he could see her now. Well, who cares? She was becoming someone she liked. She decided to let herself be lost in this experience.

Ted felt the spiritual power of their gathering and of Henry's shaman abilities. He felt totally vulnerable, all his schemes for doing away with Bagston revealed. *"How can anyone not know what I have done?"* He wanted to ask for forgiveness, but felt that he did not even deserve the asking.

As Millie sat in the darkness, she was so grateful to be here with people who loved her. It was almost like being held in their arms all at one time. Then the face of Bagston suddenly appeared before her. She gasped with fear, but was then able to contain herself.

Thelma was also seeing Bagston, but with pity now rather than with hatred. She regretted the part she felt she played in his death. Things moved so fast and now could not be undone. Thelma prayed for forgiveness and felt it happen -- something clicked in place, resolution. She sighed and cried.

"Mitakuye Oyasin! (All our relations!)" called Henry to Phil, who immediately opened the flap allowing an inrush of cool air.

"Is everyone okay?" asked Henry.

The silent calm spoke for itself. "Good. Let's do another round." Phil added one more rock at Henry's gesture, then closed the flap and they began again. "Anyone who wants to pray out loud can do so now. All are invited to do so."

Charley felt as though he ought to pray, since he was the pastor of this flock. But he felt so inadequate. He had consented to the sweat because he didn't want to seem against the healing of the harm done to the Creek nation. The whole thing was out of his religious realm. He decided he should just keep quiet.

Luther prayed -- "Grandfather! Thank you for our life and breath! Thank you for our mother the earth and the life it provides to us all -- the two-legged, the four-legged, the winged, the finned, the rock people, the creepers and the crawlers. Thank you for those here and for Henry for guiding us. Grandfather! We are nothing without you. Take pity on us and help us on our way, in the completion of our journeys."

Janice chuckled to herself, *That Luther. He's been hanging out in the woods too long."* She could not fathom Luther having any sense of the spirit. She did not know him after all.

Millie's only prayer was said silently, *Oh, Lord. Please don't let Bagston appear to me again. Why was he here? Was he going to tell everyone what she had done?"*

More silence. Henry poured more water on the rocks. The steam was hot and almost overpowering. Janice stayed in her ego, her sense of separate self and its judgments and commentary on others. She did not know how to let go, keeping herself under tight control had become her way of life.

The others had moved in their consciousness to a wider more open realm in which Henry's chanting was distant, but guiding them on to open spirit.

Time became no-time. Every breath was a prayer -- a prayer coming in to heal each one who breathed and a prayer of healing going out to "all our relations," to all life everywhere.

Charley had never prayed like this before and knew he was changed forever.

Flo began to tremble and cry. All the years of hurt and secrets came pouring out all at once. She had never known such release.

Tears ran down Jeanine's cheeks as she felt at home and at peace, something she had not allowed herself to feel for many years. Her heart glowed with gratitude.

Thelma felt all the anger she had lived with for so many years flow out of her. She was not accustomed to this feeling. She wished Junior could be there with her. But his time would come. That she was sure of.

Viola knew a high point had been reached in the sweat. She smiled. "Mitakuye Oyasin!" she called out. The sweat had done its work.

After the Sweat

Viola's kitchen was more like the reality they were accustomed to, but they were still in a state of consciousness more spacious, more open, more peaceful than ordinary reality with its schedules and demands.

Since Henry and Phil were still in the sweat lodge, Viola thought she should be the one to field questions and comments from the group. Ted, Janine, and Thelma sat at Viola's kitchen table. The others sat or stood, forming a rough circle as they drank water or sipped some of Viola's good coffee.

Each person certainly had something to say but did not want to be the first to share.

Viola allowed the silence, knowing this was a special time in each person's life -- one to be remembered for years to come. A sacred space they had experienced together but also privately.

After a time, she began to speak. "I certainly needed that quiet and holy time. My life has been so rushed and I forget I need to deliberately stop and open to its mystery. I am thankful for being here with you and sharing this time together."

Each one nodded in agreement. Just as Charley was about to share his thoughts Janice interrupted. "Luther, what was that prayer of yours about in there? Were you putting us on, or was that real for you? I never can figure you out!"

Luther looked at Janice with a grin. "There is a lot that any one of us does not know about the others. We stay locked in our own little worlds and think that others are exactly like our judgments of them."

Janice was stunned by Luther's words. She felt as though she had been exposed to the whole world. *Was he talking about me? Does he know about some of the things I've been up to?* "Well, Luther, I know that." Janice was trying to regain some of her usual superficial pose. "But, tell us what your prayer was about. Who were you praying to?"

Luther could see that Janice thought he was talking about her and only her. She was obsessed with herself to the extent of thinking that it was all about her and paradoxically, fearful that it was not about her at all.

"Well, Janice, I don't usually talk about my spiritual life. It's not for display on Oprah. But I don't mind talking about it with you here."

"I was praying to God, to the Great Mystery, the Creator, the Breather of Life Into Us All. Everyone has a name for the One who cannot be named, who is not the name we speak. The name I use is Grandfather. It is often used among the folk I sweat with. I learned it long ago."

Janice was ashamed of herself for trying to downgrade Luther, which was her usual way with everyone. He had made her realize that she did not have an exclusive relationship with God. Oh, she didn't want to admit that. Not in front of everyone here. But she suddenly felt very small.

Luther continued. "My prayer is for us all. Every being alive. Not just for the humans. I pray for all life. And everything is alive."

"I felt very alive during our sweat." The experience had given Flo a sense of security with this group of friends. She felt it safe to share herself with them. "It seemed as if a very heavy burden lifted off of me. It caused me to shed tears. Crying in front of others is something I have not allowed myself to do." As she spoke, once again tears began to run down her cheeks.

Viola gave Flo a brief hug. "One thing a sweat lodge does is soften us up."

Charley said, "It sure does. I thought I was going to melt in there!" They all laughed.

Viola grinned, "It makes us less able to keep up our pretensions and our postures. Our roles that we have adopted for ourselves are to use Charley's term, melted, stripped away."

Ted and Thelma could hardly look at each other. They knew what they had done now had to be revealed. But not here, not now.

"Anyone else want to share?" Viola wanted to be sure that everyone could say what they wished. They could not recreate this time again.

No one spoke up. Millie knew she would share with Charley when they were alone. Jeanine for once was silent. She had felt a spiritual presence during the sweat, but was still in the moment of that experience.

Ted sat with one hand partially shielding his eyes as if he was looking into a light.

Thelma knew what he was seeing, because she saw the same horror. She knew they could not keep this to themselves.

Viola saw the look exchanged between the two. "Ted, Thelma, are you okay?"

"Yeah." Ted gave a half-hearted answer.

"What exactly happened to us in there?" Jeanine couldn't hold back her questions any longer. "I didn't know what to expect when I went in. Did any of you see or hear anything while you were in there?"

"I did!" Millie's voice was louder than she expected -- a sudden release of held energy. "Did you, Jeanine?"

"What did you see, Millie?"

"Well, I saw a face. A face of someone I know or knew. It was scary. I almost screamed out. It was so real. Like he was there in front of me."

Thelma was startled. Millie said "he." -- "Was it Bagston?"

Millie dropped her head. She wished she had never said anything.

"Well, was it?" Thelma needed an answer.

"Yes! It was." Millie didn't know what kind of questions this might have stirred up from the others.

"What did you see, Jeanine?" asked Ted. "You are the one who brought it up."

"I wasn't going to say Bagston. That was the last person I was thinking of. I saw a much scarier thing. I saw myself! And I didn't like what I saw."

"Do you want to say more about that, Jeanine?" asked Viola soothingly.

"Not really. Except to say that I have spent too much time in my life looking at the lives of others, searching out their faults, and planning ways to fix them. I have never taken such a hard look at myself. It wasn't a pleasant sight."

"Bless your heart, Jeanine." Everyone looked startled to hear these words coming from Janice. "What you just said fits me to at T. I have been a real canker sore, to put it mildly. Mean, judgmental, negative about everything. That pretty much describes me. Never thought you'd hear me say that, huh? Well, it's true. It might not mean much, but I'd like to apologize to everyone here for the way I have acted toward all of you. It may be too much to ask you to forgive me."

The room was quiet. Charley spoke. "I admire your courage, Janice. I too need forgiveness. I went into the sweat lodge experience thinking I was going into a heathen ritual but was going to go along with it any way. I was a hypocrite and I judged wrongly."

"I've been more than judgmental of all of you," Luther added. "I just saw you as a bunch of hypocrites. Guess I've been just as bad as I thought you were."

Charley said, "Well, before we start holding hands and singing kumbaya here, I think we ought to help Viola clean up this kitchen."

Ted said laughingly. "We need to put a positive spin on this whole experience. Instead of feeling down on ourselves, let's be glad for what has happened. Now, who wants to wash?"

They roused themselves to the reality of stuff -- stuff that needed washing and drying and putting up, stuff that needed to be moved around, stuff that needed to be put in its proper place -- as they made small talk while restoring order to Viola's kitchen.

Ted and Thelma conversed for a moment in the hallway leading to Viola's living room, then approached Viola and asked if she had some time to talk with them the next morning. Viola was pleased. She said, "Yes. Of course."

Thelma hoped she would keep the courage she had now until the morning. It would be a relief to have the truth finally come out.

Ted's Anguish

A major plank in the Baptist spiritual practice platform was to follow your conscience rather than the dictates of the world. If you were a regenerated believer, your conscience was supposedly in tune with the mind of Christ. *If that was so,* Ted thought, *why am I so filled with anguish? That damnable sweat lodge! I wish now I had never agreed to go.*

Though for the past few months, he had an occasional emotional spasm about what he had done, Ted did not let it linger long enough to give it a name – naming it would have caused him even greater pangs.

His usual defenses were stripped away by the darkness and prayers combined with the singing and chanting of Henry Wide Bear in the intense heat.

He had it coming to him! just didn't work any more. Neither did *I had to be ruthless in order to save the church.*

The reasons for his actions which once were believable and comforting did not hold power now. *The man was the devil himself. Someone had to do something. And I was the one to do it. Now I know how Judas must have felt. But Bagston was no Christ! At least I didn't betray Jesus! Or did I?*

And then I had to bring Thelma into it too! She agreed but she never would have done what she did if I hadn't helped set it up!

Ted's conscience burned all night, keeping him awake in its flame and light. He could only pray for morning and the chance for the beginning of atonement when he and Thelma would meet with Viola.

Ted and Thelma Confess

Ted sat impatiently in Viola's office. *Thelma would be late for her own funeral!* he thought to himself. Sleepless and raw eyed, he needed to get started, to relieve himself of this burden which he had managed to bury until now. He understood now why some criminals were almost eager to confess. He wanted not only to release this pent-up energy but for someone to understand him and his actions.

He paced the floor of the little waiting room like a caged wolf.

Viola had gone down the hall to get some clean coffee cups for her morning guests. Walking into her office, she was startled to see Ted so restless. *This is not like him,* she thought. *What on earth is he going to tell me?*

Just then Thelma burst in almost running into Viola. "I'm sorry I'm late. I wasn't even sure I would come. Ted, do we really want to do this?"

Ted almost snarled at her. "Yes, Thelma, WE really want to do this! Let's get started!"

Thelma slumped down in a nearby chair, her head hung about as low as it could without her losing her balance.

Viola took Thelma by the hand and said "Good morning, Thelma! Thank you for coming in so early in the morning. Would you like a cup of coffee, a glass of water, or something?"

"I could use a cup of coffee. Thanks, Viola." With Viola's kindness shown to her, Thelma sat up and took a deep breath resolving to herself to do this even though it was going to be hard. She wanted a new life, one based on truth.

"Here you go, dear. What's this all about? Ted, I see something is really eating at your soul."

"I think I might have killed Bagston!" He let it out in one heartwrenching burst.

The silence was deafening.

Thelma just sat there with her mouth hanging open. *How could he just blurt it out like that? I thought Ted would handle this better. Now, how do we get out of this?* Thelma sobbed. She saw no way out now but full confession. "And I helped him do it."

Viola turned to Ted. "What do you mean you 'think you might have,' Ted? Why don't you and Thelma tell me what happened. Let's see if we can sort this out."

"I couldn't just stand by and let Bagston wreck the church. I had to do something."

"Okay. I can understand how you felt about Bagston. What he was doing to the church had us all upset. And I know he had some influence over your daughter after she left for Atlanta. Any father would want to strangle him. But what exactly did you do?"

Thelma interrupted. "Miss Viola, I want you to know that I didn't want to do nothing to Bagston. I hated him like everybody else did. But Ted made me do it."

Viola knew well Thelma's helpless little pawn-in-the-face-of-destiny role she adopted to keep from facing her own actions, but refused to be distracted from her focus on Ted. "Ted?"

"No one else was doing anything to stop him. I prayed about it. And got results too. The next day a package came in the mail. It was supposed to go to Bagston but somehow appeared in my post office box."

"What was in the package?"

"Viola, you know I'm not the sort to open other people's mail, but this was a direct answer to my prayer. It contained a hefty supply of Viagra from some pharmacy supply house in Canada. I sealed it back shut as best I could and put it in Bagston's home mailbox that night."

"Okay, but I don't understand how this had anything to do with Bagston's death."

"Well, Viola, you know all the town secrets. You know that I know Thelma, not just at church, but also because she knew my daughter and how Bagston had ..." Ted choked up, flooded with anger and sadness and frustration.

Thelma took over. "So Ted called me and asked me over. Said he had a plan to rid the church of Bagston once and for all."

"Ted," said Viola. "Are you able to go on with this?"

"Yes. I just feel like choking him to death with my bare hands! Even though he's dead." Ted laughs. "Guess it would do no good, choking a handful of ashes."

"There would be a long line in this town of those who would like to choke those ashes. Thelma, would you like to tell me your part in this?"

"I will, but you gotta promise me that Junior won't find out. Promise me!"

"Thelma, Junior has been understanding about a lot of hard things you have done and been through. I don't see how he could be any less forgiving about this. You know it has to all come out, don't you?"

"Oh shit! Damn it all to hell! You try to do right and what does it get you?"

"Thelma, you know what we did wasn't what you or anybody else would call right."

"Damn it, Ted! You're as bad as Bagston!"

Viola knew that profanity and anxiety went hand in hand as far as Thelma was concerned. "Thelma, calm yourself. Take a few deep breaths and think a bit before you say anything. I know you wish you hadn't been involved in this, but you were. And blaming Ted doesn't change anything. Remember you are with friends now."

"Thelma just did what I asked her to do, Viola. I explained to her that Bagston was taking Viagra, which didn't seem to surprise her a bit, and I had a suspicion that he was also heavily into cocaine."

Thelma blurted out, "He snorted coke like his nose was a Hoover."

Viola wasn't able to hold back her laughter. What a description! Thelma wasn't well educated but she had a way of getting her point across.

Ted continued, "I found on the internet that taking Viagra while doing cocaine was definitely not advisable. Heart attacks or strokes could and did happen."

Thelma told her part. "So Ted asked me if I could party it up with Bagston and make sure he kept inhaling the coke. I didn't want to have those slimy hands on me again, but I'd do anything to get back at him for what he did to me. I didn't have to worry though. He just kept talking about how wonderful he was, drinking whiskey, and doing toot. He eventually got so wired I just left. That was Saturday night. Sunday he died."

"Is that the end of your involvement, Ted?"

"Unless you call the misery I've been in involvement, Viola."

"From your point of view that would certainly be involvement. But did you do anything else to Bagston?"

"That's just it, Viola. I don't think I did anything at all to Bagston. Neither did Thelma. Bagston did it to himself. But I sure put a stain on my own soul."

"I can understand what you've been going through, both of you. And I know it hasn't been easy to talk about this. Ted, I agree with you. Bagston did this to himself. You didn't order the Viagra for him, and his cocaine habit was longstanding according to Thelma and Janice. Thelma, the most you did was to keep Bagston company while he did what was his usual practice."

"But Viola, we MEANT wrong. We meant for him to have a heart attack."

"I know you did. I think that's something you are going to have to resolve within yourselves. Evidently this was something that was going to happen to Bagston eventually. It was just a matter of time."

Ted certainly didn't feel off the hook. Viola's suggestion was something he had already thought of and dismissed. "I know what you say is true. But I feel so guilty! (laughing remorsefully) I wish now I was Catholic. They have penances to do that make them feel better. I think we Baptists are missing something there."

"You are a man of strong beliefs, Ted. You have direct access to God. He will listen to you with no judgment and with a lot more wisdom than I have."

Thelma looked confused. "I don't get what you two are talking about. All that thee-oligee just makes my head hurt. I do know this though. I have to forgive myself. I learnt that from you, Viola."

"You are right, Thelma. All of God's forgiveness can't keep you from beating yourself up about this. You do have to forgive yourself. Can you do that?"

"I done did."

Unresolved, Ted asked, "Viola do you think we need to do anything more about this?"

"What would you recommend, Ted?"

"I don't know. I guess nothing. It wouldn't do any good to confess this before the church. And none of this would be any great revelation to Janice."

Viola gave her verdict. "I think the only crime that has been committed here is a spiritual one. You both had evil intent. You wished another person's death. You even went so far as to attempt to encourage his destructive habits. Who knows? He may or may not have died that Sunday without your intent and participation. We will never know. And you will have to live with that."

"You mean Junior won't have to know?"

"That's up to you and Ted."

Henry Wide Bear's Sermon

The church was packed. Henry Wide Bear walked to the pulpit and began to speak. His Creek features were in sharp contrast with the predominately Anglo audience.

"I ask for blessings on our meeting here tonight. I ask that the ears of our hearts be open, that we can hear what our Maker keeps telling us, that though we are each different we are all members of the Navel

Tribe. We are all plucked from the same vine and we have the belly scars to prove it."

"We do, Mommy! Look!" blurted out a small boy captivated by Henry's words. Laughter rippled around the room.

Henry smiled to himself. *And a little child shall lead them,* he thought.

"I have already met many of you. (The sweat lodge participants smiled.) But I have not said what I need to say. This church is built on sacred ground, but maybe not in the way you think. It is built on the bones of my people. Your church is built on a Creek burial ground."

"For those of you who want to look at the evidence, the church Board of Trustees has the complete information." Henry allowed time for the murmurings and whisperings to subside. "I am here tonight to tell you two things. It's alright. And it's alright.

"But first you need to know that the world is more mysterious than you may admit. After all, the Christian Holy Book is full of strange things, like axe heads floating on water, donkeys talking, tongues of fire coming down on people's heads, to name a few. You may say that is metaphor or that happened way back then. We live in a different time now. Not so. We still live in mystery where the miraculous is natural and what we call the super natural is more real than Wall Street. But then most everything is more real than Wall Street."

Folk laughed. They were warming to Henry's quiet, simple, and humorously honest way of speaking.

"All of us humans as peoples, tribes, groups, nations have inflicted harm on each other. To simply list all our harms and grievances would take all night and more and still would get us nowhere. I tell you one story about this. I was at a gathering of some of the Lakota Sioux people up in South Dakota. This very old Lakota man with a deeply wrinkled face stood up and spoke at length in his native tongue. As he spoke there was much nodding of heads. Though I do not speak Lakota, I noticed he would often speak the same phrase or sentence. He sat down seemingly satisfied that his message was received. I asked a friend afterward, "What did the elder say?" "He was passing something on from the 1800's about the U. S. Government. He had been entrusted with this information from his kin before him. He said, 'They still haven't paid us for those horses!'"

"So you see, your native brothers and sisters have a Wall Street too!" The congregation laughed with appreciation and understanding. "We have all wronged each other. As it says in the Holy Book, we have all sinned and come short of the glory of God."

"I come back to the two alrights I mentioned. When my people were forced to leave these lands many years ago before any of us were born, a Creek shaman, what some of you might call a medicine man, blessed this burial site with a blessing so profound that if anything profane violated it, the energies of the profane would turn against itself and destroy itself."

"You know what profane means, don't you? It comes from two words **pro**, meaning outside of, and **fanum**, temple. Profane means outside the temple, outside the sacred.

"And that is what happened here. A profane heart, a heart living outside the temple of the sacred, contaminated this church. It was only a matter of time that the profanity rebounded upon itself and destroyed itself."

"But that's alright now. The profanity is gone. That's the first alright."

"The second alright is that it is alright now that this church exists atop my people's burying ground. I have met with some of your church leaders and together we prayed and asked for forgiveness and cleansing of ourselves and of past wrongs. We prayed long and hard and with deep sincerity and pain of heart until we knew our prayers were answered. The blessing on the burial ground is still here, but it is a blessing and not a curse. As you work to make this church a blessing, the two blessings will combine and produce a powerful force. A force for good."

"So we have the two alrights. Can you say alright?"

The congregation caught by surprise did pretty well but not their best: "Alright!"

Henry chuckled. He said, "Okay. That's the first alright. There is one more. Can you say alright?" The congregation gave full voice. "ALRIGHT!"

Henry sat down, his work done.

Security Check-In

Luther signaled the waitress, Lu Ella (Bobby Joe's sister on his mother's side), for another cup of coffee. "Charley, I just want to let you know that your church money helped provide some of the boys with at least a month's supply of marihoochie, innumerable twelve-packs, and some all-nighters in the Phoenix City titty bars."

"Luther, I don't want to hear about it."

"And some are sporting new tattoos, one even has Jesus crucified on a cross on his back. So you may have a new convert there."

"Will you stop it! I came here prepared to thank you for the good job you and the others did in providing security for us at the preach-off and now all I want to do is bean you with my coffee cup."

"Mission accomplished!" Luther flashed his sardonic smile and leaned back in his chair. "Somebody has to bring you out of that dream world you live in."

They sipped their early morning coffee and sat pleasantly relaxed. The town was coming back to normal after the deluge of newscasters, journalists, preachers, singers, choirs, musicians, soothsayers, doom predictors, necromancers, and assorted metaphysicists of various persuasions.

The town dog had resumed his position in the middle of the street where everyone carefully drove around him. The pigeons were back on their perch – the head and shoulders and outstretched sword of the confederate war memorial general on horseback. Older men were on the benches in front of the courthouse playing checkers and whittling sticks to nothingness with their sharply honed pocket knives.

"I guess Mayhew decided to lay low since his henchmen are locked up in our county jail. The only trouble we had during the preach-off was with some of the granny women in your church complaining that someone was sitting in their seat. It was always an outlander who didn't understand small town etiquette. We made sure they got a lesson pretty quickly."

"Luther, you didn't ….!"

"Don't jump to judgment so quickly, preacher boy! We were polite but firm."

"Preacher boy? It's just that I know how you heathen pagans are, Luther!"

Luther laughed. "There's hope for you yet, Charley."

Out On A Limb

The Angel of Fire and the Angel of Light sat in a tree overlooking the wide flowing river, trees being traditional resting places of Angels assigned to earth. Only the most observant of humans could see them and even then would only see small shimmerings of light, unless the Angels decided differently.

Right now they had assumed the shape of a small boy and girl, two of their favorite manifestations because of their innocence and honesty and wide-eyed understanding.

"Well, do you think they learned their lesson?" said the Fire. Giggling poured out of the Light that matched the gurgling of the river. "No." He swung his legs dangling from the branch and peered closely at an eagle flying overhead.

"Why should they?" he continued. "They are on a journey, an incredible journey that they do not believe or even grasp much of the time. They are made of dirt, you know."

"Yes, but the Sublime One Himself breathed fire and air and light into them. Why doesn't that part take hold?" The Fire Angel already knew the answer but liked to hear Light talk. Besides, the Fire Angel's job was one of condensed fierceness while the Angel of Light belonged to a Brotherhood that flowed through the universe with instantaneous contact and communion with all.

"You know the answer. This is a dualistic universe. Look at the way they are physically built. They have "on the one hand" and "on the other hand" and the left hand doesn't know what the right is doing. Sometimes they work at odds, sometimes they move as one."

"Yes," said the Fire Angel. "Their brains are the same way – two chunks fused. You know how they blurt out sometimes 'I've got half a mind.'?"

"Yes. One of their country western songs says something like 'I've got half a mind to leave you but half a heart to go.'"

They both laughed and watch the colorings in the sky as the sun disappears behind the earth horizon. The air goes still. Ducks fly across the river heading for their evening place of rest.

"Well, I guess we better get back over there." "Yep. There's no telling what they are up to by now."